Brothers in Blood

As young Stubbs 'Sunshine' Shining is riding West he hears shooting, and sees four gunmen firing at a homestead. He fires a couple of shots to scare them off, and discovers that the person defending the property is a middle-aged woman named Bethany Bartok. She invites Sunshine in and gives him food and drink. He learns that her husband has died, her son Bart has gone off in search of his fortune, and her daughter Elspeth has travelled East to be educated. Sunshine decides to stay on at the farm for a short spell. But soon things get complicated. Bart has been kidnapped and the local Cutaway brothers are determined to get their hands on the property for some reason. Then Sunshine becomes even more deeply involved in the fate of the Bartok homestead when Bethany's daughter Elspeth returns.

Sunshine soon gets a reputation as a gunfighter, but that's only the beginning. Why do the Cutaway brothers want the farm? Who is holding young Bart captive? And where is he being held? Sunshine starts to untangle the thread that leads him into very dangerous territory.

Brothers in Blood

Lee Lejeune

A Black Horse Western

ROBERT HALE

© Lee Lejeune 2017
First published in Great Britain 2017

ISBN 978-0-7198-2165-3

The Crowood Press
The Stable Block
Crowood Lane
Ramsbury
Marlborough
Wiltshire SN8 2HR

www.bhwesterns.com

Robert Hale is an imprint
of The Crowood Press

Typeset by
Derek Doyle & Associates, Shaw Heath
Printed and bound in Great Britain by
CPI Group (UK) Ltd, Croydon, CR0 4YY

CHAPTER ONE

His name was Stubbs – Stubbs Shining. Back home they had called him 'Sunshine' because he had a smile for everyone, including the town bullies. But now there were no bullies and nobody in particular to bother him . . . or so he thought. He was just a young *hombre* riding West in search of . . . well, in search of what? He had no idea what he was looking for, and he had nobody to talk things over with except his horse Chingalong, who wasn't much of a conversationalist either. Chingalong was just a plain chestnut with a white blaze on his nose, his main virtue being that he didn't argue a man's head off.

'Now lookee here, Chingalong,' Sunshine said to the horse, 'I'm real disappointed in you. I thought we were travelling West in search of our fortune, or at least something to interest a man, and what do we get? Cold nights and days to roast your balls off. This really isn't good enough, you know. You've got to use your horse sense to get us into those good green pastures you promised me. You hear me, hoss?'

Chingalong just tossed his head and plodded on through the wild undulating country towards the distant blue hills.

'You know what?' Sunshine continued. 'A man could go

plumb crazy out here, riding to nowhere in particular.'

Chingalong pricked up his ears but still said nothing.

'What's that you hear?' Shining asked him, but the next second he heard it for himself, the *crack-crack-crack* of gunfire somewhere over to the right.

'Sounds like someone's shooting deer or prairie chickens,' Shining said to himself. He reined in and listened more intently. 'That doesn't sound too much like deer-hunting, though,' he added. 'Sounds more like people – shooting to me. Maybe we should keep clear. What do you think, hoss?'

Chingalong raised his head and twitched his ears.

'Well, you're probably right at that,' Sunshine agreed. 'On the other hand, maybe we should look into this matter a little more closely. After all, you don't know what you'll find unless you look, do you?' He jigged Chingalong round to the right and headed towards the bluff, beyond which there was some kind of gully. As he drew towards the edge of the gully the sound of the gunfire got sharper; he could hear shouting too and it didn't sound too friendly either. He dismounted and drew his Winchester carbine out of its saddle holster.

'You stay right here,' he said to Chingalong. 'Just chew on that patch of grass over there while I take a looksee.'

He walked to the brow of the hill and looked over it into the valley below. What he saw surprised him: a farmstead and a corral. Nothing unusual about that. But there were four horsemen and they weren't shooting deer; they were firing their weapons at the windows of the homestead and someone inside was firing back.

'This is a bad situation,' Sunshine said to himself. 'You don't want to get yourself in too deep here. It could be like sticking your head in a noose.' He had always thought discretion to be the better part of valour. At least that was what

6

his ma had always said and she was about the wisest woman he had known so far. Just then one of the riders started hurling abuse at the homesteader inside the main cabin.

'You gonna come right out and face the music, you yellow-bellied skunks?'

It wasn't what was said but the snarling way the man threw it at the cabin that made the hairs at the back of Sunshine's neck stand on end.

Then someone shouted back from inside the cabin; it was a woman's voice. Sunshine couldn't hear the exact words but he judged by the tone that she said something like:

'Leave good folk alone to go about their business, you cowardly vinegarroons!'

What in heck's a vinegarroon? Sunshine wondered. That woman might not know how to shoot straight, but she sure knows how to fire off with her tongue; though her voice was rough and somewhat jagged at the edges she sounded as brave as an eagle sheltering her chicks.

The gunmen laughed and opened fire again. For Sunshine it was that heartless laugh that settled matters. So he got down on his belly, pushed the Winchester ahead of him and levered a shell into place.

Should I shoot at them or above them? he wondered. He had never fired a shot in anger but his old man had taught him to shoot straight at tin cans perched on the fence back home.

'You've got a good eye, my son,' Jed Shining had said. 'You might not be the heaviest sonofagun but you can box and shoot. So you can always defend yourself in any scrape you find yourself in.' That was how Jed Shining measured a man.

The gunmen were just about within range and, taking account of the trajectory, Sunshine might have brought one of them down. But he decided to aim just above the head of the one who had snarled at the woman. So, without thinking further on the matter, he aimed just to the right of the *hombre* and fired. Then he shifted his aim and fired above the head of another of the gunmen.

'That'll give those mean *hombres* something to think about,' he said to himself.

The effect was instantaneous. The gunman wheeled round to face in Sunshine's direction.

'We've got company, boys,' he croaked in surprise.

'What in hell's name. . . !' one of the other gunmen shouted.

Then there came another blast from inside the cabin and the woman shouted:

'Get out of here, you whey-bellies, before I come right out and fix up you good and proper.'

'OK, boys,' the leader said. 'We've done enough for now.' He wheeled his horse round and made for the surrounding scrub. The others followed, peering up at the ridge where Sunshine lay concealed.

'Don't be fooled,' Sunshine said to himself. 'Those mean bastards could ride round and try to bushwhack me.' He drew back from the ridge and made towards Chingalong.

Chingalong was still chewing contentedly on the patch of grass.

'Hold still while I mount up,' Sunshine advised him.

He rode out through the cut-leaf birches and peered in the direction the four riders had taken. He could see them riding away to the west.

'OK,' he said to Chingalong. 'Now we go down and and hold a little powwow with that good woman.'

He rode over the ridge and down towards the homestead. As he drew closer a woman threw open the door and stepped out under the overhang. She was holding a buffalo gun. She had grey hair and steely grey eyes and she didn't look any too pleased to see him.

'Don't come any closer,' she said menacingly. 'I'm just about sick of your tricks. I'm staying right here and you can stick that in your pipe and smoke it.'

Sunshine noticed that, in fact, she did have a small stub of pipe clamped between her teeth.

He drew rein and raised his hands.

'Yes, ma'am,' he said. 'Just as long as you stop pointing that gun at me, I have no quarrel with anything you say.'

The woman, who must have been aged about fifty, squinted at him down the barrel of her buffalo gun.

'What do you want here?' she asked.

Sunshine nodded and gave her one of his most disarming smiles.

'I was just passing through, ma'am. I have no quarrel with any man – or woman for that matter. I just heard shooting and I stopped to take a looksee. Then I fired a couple of shots to put the frighteners on those gun-toting scaramouches.'

She squinted at him for a moment longer and decided he was probably harmless. Then she lowered the buffalo gun a little.

'You a stranger in these parts?' she asked.

'Just riding through,' he said. 'Didn't like the sound of those scaramouches shooting off their mouths and their guns in your direction. So I handed out a spoonful of their own medicine. By the way, what does whey-face mean?'

The woman stared at him for a moment, then grinned.

'I don't rightly know what a whey-face is. It's just an expression I use from time to time, 'specially when I see that Brad Bassington around here.'

'I guess he must be the one who was shovelling all that

9

shit in your direction, if you'll pardon the language.'

'That's the one. Pity you missed him with that peashooter of yours.'

Sunshine shrugged. 'Didn't aim to hit him. Never shot a man in my life. Just wanted to scare those scaramouches off before they did any real damage apart from breaking windows.'

She grinned again. 'Well, you'd better come inside if you can spare the time. That hoss of yourn looks like he can do with a rest.'

'That's mighty civilized of you, ma'am. Chingalong will be grateful for that. He's the best hoss I know. The only friend I've got, right now.'

He took Chingalong into the barn and then walked into the cabin.

Inside it was surprisingly neat and tidy. Everything seemed to have a place and every place had a something.

The woman put her buffalo gun on a rack, where it obviously belonged with several other weapons, and folded her arms. She was old by Sunshine's standards but she had an eagle-like gleam in her eye.

'Take a good look round,' she said in that croaky voice of hers, 'because you won't be staying long.'

Sunshine nodded and smiled.

'That's all right by me because I don't aim to stick around either.'

The woman held her head on one side and took the stubby pipe out from between her teeth.

'Where you headed, son?' she asked.

'Like I said, nowhere in particular. I'm just riding through the territory. But I'm not sure where exactly I'm headed. It depends on the circumstances and what I find.'

The woman nodded thoughtfully.

'Guess I ought to thank you for taking a shot at those sidewinding critters.'

'It was a pleasure, ma'am. I'd do the same thing again if I had to.'

'With that kind of attitude, you're likely either to get a bellyful of lead or a reputation as a shootist, 'cause it's shoot or get shot out here. You ought to know that before someone shoots your head off your shoulders.'

'Well, I don't aim to be a shootist or get my head shot off my shoulders,' he said. 'So I guess that's why I'm moving on.'

She gave him a long shrewd look. 'How old are you, son?'

'Just a little bit younger than my back teeth and about as old as my toes,' he said.

She gave a grunt of appreciation. 'What's your name?'

'Name's Stubbs Shining but most folks call me Sunshine.'

She screwed up her lips. 'Sounds sort of girlish.'

'Well, ma'am, every man has his feminine side. It's what makes us human, you know.'

She grinned at him through those keen grey eyes.

'You educated, Sunshine?'

He was silent for a moment, then said, 'I've been to school, if that's what you mean. I didn't set much store by it, but I learned how to read and do my calculations. So I get by.'

She nodded several times, each time more affirmatively.

'Now,' she said, 'why don't you set yourself down at the table so I can feed you up some. Least I can do considering you saw off those gunslinging desperadoes.'

'Thank you, ma'am.' He took off his wide-brimmed hat and hung it on a hook provided for the purpose. His hair was long and fair and came almost down to his shoulders.

11

'Looks like you can do with a haircut,' she said with a tinge of mockery.

'Been thinking about dropping in on a barber if I could find one,' he replied.

'There's a barber in town. Calls himself Close Shave. He's also the funeral director. So I wouldn't recommend him too highly.' She drew off a pint of what she called home brew and set in front of him. 'Drink that down and you can forget about all your troubles.'

'Thank you, ma'am.' Sunshine sipped at the home brew. It was bitter and had a kick, if not exactly like a mule at least like a small pony. The woman grinned at him.

'I see you like it. Wait till you taste the stew.' She cackled like a witch and went to a primitive stove where a large black pot was bubbling away. She dished out a generous helping and placed it before him.

'Thank you, ma'am,' he said. 'I might change my mind and stay awhile after all.'

She drew back a chair and sat across from him.

'Before you ask,' she said, 'I'm Bethany Bartok and I'm old enough to be your ma. Does that answer your questions?'

'Well, since I didn't ask any questions, it'll have to do,' he answered between mouthfuls. 'By the way, the stew's even better than you promised.' He looked up and saw that she was staring at him with curiosity. 'You want to tell me what you're doing living out here alone with no neighbours for miles around? And why those men were gunning down on you like that?' he asked.

Then she told him her story. Several years earlier she had moved into the locality with her husband Bart and their two children, Elspeth and Bart Junior. They had liked the small town of Logan and had decided to put down roots in a place close by. Then a man called Timberlane had offered them the property at a fair price and they had taken it in all innocence.

'I say "in all innocence",' Bethany explained, 'because at that time we had no idea that the Cutaways practically owned the town and the range all around it.'

'Who would the Cutaways be?' Sunshine asked.

Bethany considered for a moment, choosing the right words.

'The Cutaway brothers are two of the most ornery critters you can expect to meet in the territory. They're cattle ranchers and they're as rich as that Greek guy in ancient times whose touch turned everything to gold.'

'So what's with these brothers, apart from they're as rich as Croesus?'

'What's with them is they want this property, that's what's with them. They offered me money but this is my home, so I turned it down. Now they're using those danged gunslingers to scare me off. Except I don't scare that easy.'

Sunshine had finished his stew and his pint of home brew; now he just wanted to sit back and relax for the rest of the day. It was like the woman had cast some kind of spell on him and he expected her to turn into a fair maiden any time soon.

'So why do those Cutaways want to get their hands on the property?' he asked in a slightly sleepy tone. Bethany Bartok creased her brow in thought.

'I don't know the answer to that, Sunshine. Could be they think there's gold or a seam of silver on the property. I did hear rumours but I've never seen any sign. On the other hand it might just be that they think of the whole range as theirs. So they want me out. Does that make sense?'

Sunshine nodded. 'It could do. You never can know what folks think even if they tell you, can you? But there must be something that interests them if they send men to gun down on you like that. Stands to reason, doesn't it?'

She gave a slow nod. 'You could be right. You sure got a head on your shoulders, sonny.'

'It ain't much,' he said modestly, 'but I try to use it best I can.' He looked around him. 'You got everything neat and tidy here, ma'am. You mentioned your husband and two children. How come you're here on your own?'

She picked up her stubby pipe and stared at it as though it held the answer to all known questions.

'I'm here on my own because they've all lit out for the hills, so to speak.'

'What? All three of them?' he asked in surprise.

'In a manner of speaking, yes. My girl Elspeth went back East with some folks she knew, to study, and my boy Bart Junior decided he didn't like life on the farm, so he went off some place to make his fortune.'

'So, what about Bart Senior?' Sunshine asked.

She was silent while she stuffed her pipe with some kind of tobacco. Then she said:

'Unfortunately, Bart Senior took sick and died. He was a good man but nature dealt him out a bad hand and now he's in the land of eternal happiness ... or so the preacher said.'

Sunshine frowned. 'That must have been difficult for you. I hope he likes it there.'

She raised an eyebrow. 'Life is difficult, sonny. That's one lesson you have to learn.'

Sunshine didn't reply. He knew already that life could be difficult.

After she had lit her stubby pipe again, she gave him a

scrutinizing look.

'That's my story. Now spill out the beans on yourn.'

'There isn't a whole lot to spill out. My old man was a small-time trader and my ma had taught school. I was the only son. I think I came as something of a surprise to them when I arrived.'

'So why did you leave?'

Sunshine grinned. 'Well, I just left. I can't give a good reason. I guess I'm something of a restless spirit. Not good enough to be a scholar and not strong enough to be a labouring man. I thought of going to sea but then some-body offered me my good hoss Chingalong, and I took it as a sign. I decided to ride West and see what life has to offer in this strange land . . . and that's why I'm here.'

Bethany puffed out a small cloud of blueish smoke.

'So you have no particular plans for the future?'

He shrugged. 'I'm not sure I believe in plans. You make a plan and something comes along to bust it apart.'

She continued smoking for a while. Then:

'I might put a proposition to you, young man.'

'Well, I'm always open to suggestions. So why don't you spill it out, Mrs Bartok?'

She looked thoughtfully at her pipe.

'Why don't you stay here for a while, maybe a week? I can't offer you anything to speak of, other than food and drink.'

'That sounds acceptable,' he said. 'What would I do in return?'

She shrugged. 'You could talk good sense to me and renew the windows those hoodlums shot out. There's always something a body can do around here.'

Sunshine smiled. 'You just made an offer I can't refuse,' he said.

CHAPTER TWO

After what had been a busy day and with a bellyful of good stew and home-brewed beer, Sunshine fell into a deep sleep. But it wasn't dreamless. He dreamed that a whole host of gunmen were coming at him from all directions. He was trying to bring his Winchester carbine into play but one of the gunmen reached out and grabbed it and bent it in half just like it was made of putty. Sunshine woke up shouting, then fell into a deep sleep again.

Next thing he knew, a light was shining in his eyes. When he opened them he saw that a beautiful young woman was standing at the end of his bed.

'Where am I?' he asked. The next second the beautiful young woman had transmogrified into Bethany Bartok.

'Time you shook the sleep-dust out of your eyes, young man,' she croaked. Sunshine sat up quickly; then he remembered.

'Is it late?' he asked as the sun streamed into his eyes.

'Late enough,' she said. 'I've been up at least two hours and I'm good and ready to get my mouth round a wholesome breakfast. You want to join me you'd better get your pants on soldier fashion: double quick. Or you could come in your underpants. It don't make no never mind to me.' She went to the door, cackled and turned.

'You want to clean up you'd better get down to the creek. There's good running water there and the fish seem to like it, but I wouldn't recommend it if you suffer from goose pimples. I could heat up a bath for you next Saturday week if that's to your taste.' Then she went away, cackling again, leaving the door ajar.

Sunshine hopped out of bed and pulled on his shirt and pants double quick. Then he went into the outer room, where he caught the rich smell of frying ham and eggs. Bethany turned from the primitive stove where she was working a minor miracle.

'You made the right choice, son,' she said. 'Sit yourself down and have a good hearty breakfast: ham and pancakes. Eat up good 'cause we've got a long day ahead of us.'

Sunshine sat down at table and, from the noises his stomach made, he judged it thought it was in food heaven.

'You still hungry?' the old woman asked.

'I can sure eat a little,' he conceded.

'Coffee too,' she said. 'We don't drink home brew in the morning in case we fall asleep on the job.'

'What's the plan?' Sunshine asked as he prepared to stuff a portion of pancake into his mouth.

'We don't have plans,' she said. 'We just have ideas. My idea is we go into town and fix ourselves up with glass to patch up the windows those deadbeats shot out yesterday.'

'Is town far?' he asked.

'No more than a mile. There's other supplies I need too.'

'How do we get there?'

'We go in by buckboard. I might be pretty poor but I'm not dirt poor – and I've got something else you might like to look at.' She reached into a drawer and pulled out what looked like a whole bundle of leather. 'You ever handled one of these afore?' She put the bundle on the table in front of him and he saw it was a handgun in a holster.

'What's this?' he said.

'This is a Colt Peacemaker revolver,' she said, 'with a holster and a cartridge belt. Could be handy if we get into a scrape.'

'Where did you get it?'

'That's for me to know.' She tapped her nose with an index finger.

'What d'you want me to do with it?'

'You just strap it round your waist and look important. Folks see you wearing it they'll think you're a gunman – or at least you mean business.'

Sunshine looked at her in surprise.

'If folks think I'm a gunman they might call me out. That could be dangerous, you know.'

Bethany nodded. 'You got a point there, Sunshine. We don't want you to get yourself killed before your time, do we? So I suggest we keep it hidden under a blanket in the buckboard. How would that be?'

Sunshine agreed that might be a whole lot better.

Together they measured up the broken windows. After that they harnessed the horses to the buckboard.

'I guess I'll ride Chingalong and you can drive the buckboard,' Sunshine said.

'That's OK by me,' Bethany said.

Chingalong was bright-eyed and ready for action after a well-earned rest and it didn't take long to get into town. Sunshine saw that Logan wasn't much of a town, though there were a few stores with pots and pans hanging up in the windows. He noticed the barber shop too, with a pole of red and white stripes above the door and a sign that said CLOSE SHAVE BARBER'S and, underneath, *Come in, we do you good.*

Bethany drew up outside the most important-looking

store and climbed down on to the sidewalk.

'This is where we get the glass,' she told Sunshine. 'Keep hold of that Winchester of yourn,' she added. 'Maybe you should stock up on shells in case we meet those scaramouches again.'

They walked into the store and Sunshine looked around. There was a smell of leather and polish and many other indefinable odours. The storekeeper was invisible behind a newsheet.

'Morning, Mrs Bartok,' his voice chimed out. 'What can I get you on this good sunny morning?' He lowered the newsheet and peered at Sunshine through small specs at the end of his nose. 'Ah, so you got yourself a new assistant, Mrs Bartok?'

Bethany grunted. 'This is Sunshine,' she said.

'Well, that's a good name to have,' the storekeeper observed, greeting Sunshine with a smile. 'Got a good cheery smile to match, too. Good morning, Sunshine.' He nodded and stood up behind the counter. 'You come from far, Mr Sunshine?'

Sunshine smiled. 'Just passing through, mister.'

'Some kind of tumbleweed. Would that be right?'

'It might be so,' Sunshine said. 'Depends what a man finds, doesn't it?'

'The way you talk, you sound like an educated man,' the storekeeper said.

'I did have a little schooling,' Sunshine admitted. 'Didn't take to it too well. So I decided to strike out West.'

'Well now, Mr Snaze,' Bethany suddenly intervened, 'maybe you'd care to look down my list and see if you can oblige.'

Snaze turned to Bethany and gave her a toothy grin.

'Why, of course, that would be my pleasure, ma'am. Why don't you just set yourself down and have yourself a mug of that fresh coffee my good lady brews up.'

As if by magic a somewhat lean and hungry-looking woman appeared from the back room.

'Why, good morning, Mrs Bartok,' she said heartily, giving Sunshine a passing glance. 'Please come through. It's a real pleasure to see you.'

The two women disappeared through a curtain from behind which Sunshine heard the sound of chatter and laughter, mostly from Mrs Snaze. They say fat people are more talkative and cheerful than thin people, but Mrs Snaze certainly wasn't fat.

Mr Snaze peered at Bethany's list through his small specs, grunting and saying 'yes', 'yes', and 'I've got some out back'. Then he looked up at Sunshine.

'See Mrs Bartok's got glass listed here, with the size. Would that be window glass?'

Sunshine nodded. 'That would be window glass, Mr Snaze. Did you have any other kind?'

Snaze chuckled. 'Well, there's glass and glass, Mr Sunshine.'

'In that case you'd better make it the toughest you've got. Bullet proof would be best.'

The storekeeper peered at Sunshine through his specs.

'Bullet proof,' he muttered. 'We don't have bullet proof. We just have ordinary window glass.' He glanced at the door of the shop and then back at Sunshine. 'Are you telling me someone took a shot at the Bartok place and broke a window?'

Sunshine grinned. 'I'm not telling you anything, Mr Snaze. I'm just ordering glass for a broken window – two, in fact.'

'Hm,' Snaze said. 'I'll just go out back and see what I've got in stock. If you'll be kind enough to keep an eye on the shore.'

'Be glad to, Mr Snaze. Thanks for the honour.'

Snaze raised an eyebrow and went through to the back of the store.

Sunshine retrieved the Winchester carbine he'd left on a chair and went to the door. Through the window he could see all the people walking and riding by. He looked towards Bethany's buckboard and then at Chingalong at the hitching rail. As he watched a man approached Chingalong and started running his hand over the horse's back, as though he was assessing him for the knacker's yard. Sunshine stepped out on to the sidewalk.

The man turned slowly and glanced in his direction; something about him looked vaguely familiar. Then a memory slotted into Sunshine's brain. *Why,* he thought, *unless I'm a Dutchman, that's one of the* hombres *that was gunning down on the Bartok place yesterday.*

As if by thought transference, the man turned towards him.

'Is this your hoss, sonny?'

Sunshine stiffened. 'What's that to you, Granddad?'

A wave of black anger passed across the man's face, which wasn't exactly handsome in the first place.

'Did I hear you right?' he snarled.

Sunshine shook his head.

'That depends on what you heard.'

The man mounted the sidewalk and took a step in Sunshine's direction. Sunshine gave him an appraising look. The man was maybe four or five inches taller than Sunshine and twice as heavy. He wore a black vest and a handgun low on his hip.

'So,' the man said, 'we've got a real blabbermouth here. Did someone tell you you need a haircut, sonny?'

Sunshine smiled. 'Matter of fact someone mentioned it

21

only yesterday.'

'Well, sonny – or is it missy – I can't make up my mind—'

'You don't have to, Granddad, since it's none of your business.'

The man's face went dark purple with rage.

'Oh, I think it is my business all right, since I'm gonna shove that pretty face of yourn right down into that drink trough here and if you happen to drown in the process that will be just too bad.'

The prospect looked decidedly ugly. The big man took a step or two closer to Sunshine and Sunshine knew there was only one choice: he could either face being ducked in the horse trough or use the pugilistic skills he had learned back home. He stood quite still as the bully came right up to him and reached out with his right hand to seize Sunshine by the collar.

Sunshine was light and very fast; he ducked to one side and brought his fist into the big man's belly. It wasn't the heaviest of blows but the bully gave a grunt of pain and surprise. Before he could draw back Sunshine crouched low, grabbed the man's arm, then swung his own right leg so that bully fell forward and sideways against the horse trough. He hung there momentarily before disappearing over the side with a huge splash.

Sunshine stood for a moment trying to get his breath back, but he knew he was in better shape than his opponent. The man had disappeared into the horse trough; now he rose spluttering and spewing out water. Sunshine reached for the Stetson that had fallen into the trough and jammed it on the man's head. Then he pushed the man down into the trough again.

'Did I hear you mention a haircut, Granddad?' he wheezed.

There were roars of laughter from all around. Sunshine

drew back from the trough and picked up the Winchester he had cast aside. He became aware of the crowd that had assembled to watch the fracas. Among them was Bethany Bartok; she was holding the Peacemaker and pointing it at the bully in the trough.

'Get away from the trough,' she said to Sunshine.

'Yes, ma'am,' he agreed.

As the bully sat in the trough with his wet Stetson perched on his head and water cascading down his face everyone laughed; nobody stretched out a hand to help him.

'How in heaven's name did you do that?' someone asked Sunshine.

'It just sort of came naturally,' Sunshine said with due modesty.

'Well now, you're not just a pretty face, Sunshine,' Bethany said. 'You've sure proved that and I guess they're not gonna like it one little bit.'

Sunshine was quite wet from the splash but fortunately the sun was fully out and ready to dry him.

'You got everything on your list?' he asked her.

'I think that's everything I need – with a bonus,' she said.

Mr and Mrs Snaze were loading everything on to the buckboard, taking care to wrap the window glass in a blanket.

'My word and glory be!' Mrs Snaze said. 'How did that saddle bum get into the trough? Did a horse duck him in there?'

That caused another round of laughter. The storekeeper, who was somewhat prone to exaggeration, spoke up.

'I seen it all, every move. That Sunshine ain't as sunny

as he looks. For such a small guy he's almost as strong as Samson himself.'

'Must be the hair,' someone volunteered.

'What have you been eating, boy?' another man asked. Bethany held out the Peacemaker.

'Here, take this, Sunshine. I guess you've earned it.'

Sunshine held up his hand. 'Thanks a lot, Bethany, but first I must help my friend out of the bath.'

More laughter.

The bully now had his hands on the sides of the trough. Sunshine took hold of his arm to steady him.

'Let me give you a hand, my friend.'

'Keep away from me, boy,' the bully grunted. He crawled out on to the sidewalk, stood up shakily and shook himself like a wet dog. Then he reached down for his gun.

'Don't do that, mister, unless you want to find yourself in the drink again,' Sunshine warned him.

The bully took Sunshine's measure and shook his head.

'I'll get you for this, missy,' he growled.

'Don't bother, Granddad,' Sunshine said. 'Put the whole thing down to experience.'

'Good morning, folks,' a voice said. 'What seems to be the trouble here?'

'Good morning, Sheriff,' Snaze the storekeeper replied. 'Nothing to worry about. Just a little horseplay. It's all over now.'

'*Horse*play?' someone echoed. 'That's real neat!'

Yet more laughter.

'This is Sheriff McGiven,' Bethany introduced. 'This here is Stubbs Shining, Sheriff. Likes to be called Sunshine.'

'Well, it's good to meet you, Sunshine. I didn't see what

happened but you sure gave Slam Smith a dunking.'

'Didn't have a whole lot of choice,' Sunshine said. 'It was him or me and I prefer to have my bath less publicly.'

The sheriff grinned. He was somewhat stout but he stood up straight and tall.

'Well, that's OK, just as long as you realize Slam isn't gonna be any too pleased – and neither will the Cutaway brothers. Did you have any other business in town?'

'I think that's just about everything,' Bethany said. 'Time we moseyed on home before the clouds bring down thunder and lightning.'

Since there wasn't a cloud in the sky that remark gave rise to more laughter. Clearly Bethany Bartok was regarded as a local funster. Sunshine ran his hand down Chingalong's neck and mounted up.

'You hear all that shenanigans, Ching? Don't worry yourself too much on that account, and don't let it spoil your thirst either. We can find some other water hole further along the trail – and I guess it will be a lot purer.'

He swung Chingalong away from the hitching line and on to Main Street. Most of the townsfolk had gone about their business but one or two were still hanging about, grinning and laughing up at Sunshine.

'Where did you learn those fancy tricks?' someone asked.

'I learned them at the feet of the Great Lama of Oz,' Sunshine replied as he swung Chingalong alongside Bethany's buckboard.

'Who in the name of heaven is the Great Lama of Oz?' Bethany asked, putting a flame to her stubby pipe.

'Oh, he's just a guy who lives up there in those storm clouds you mentioned just now,' Sunshine told her with a smile.

*

As they jogged on down the trail towards the homestead Bethany had her pipe clenched firmly between her teeth, but she wasn't smiling. Sunshine noticed she kept her buffalo gun close beside her. His Winchester was now in its saddle holster but he had the gunbelt strapped to his side, with the Colt Peacemaker handy.

'You ever used a handgun before?' Bethany asked him from the corner of her mouth.

'No, I never have. I practised with the Winchester a few times but I guess it isn't too difficult.'

'The technicalities are different,' she said. 'When we get back to the spread you'd better put up a few bean cans and take some pot shots, but don't aim for the windows or we might need to go back to the store.' She chuckled in her own semi-masculine way. 'By the way, I thought you did remarkable well with that bully Slam Smith. He always picks on someone smaller than himself, or someone he can outshoot. But he made a big mistake in your case. Lucky for you he didn't manage to pull that gun of his.'

'That wasn't luck. That was good judgement on your part. Would you have used this Peacemaker?'

'I would have done if I had to but I might have winged one of the horses if I had.'

'Unless I'm mistaken that Slam Smith was one of the *hombres* gunning down on you yesterday.'

'I guess you're right on that,' she said.

'Did he ever shoot a man?' Sunshine asked. Bethany nodded grimly.

'Shot a man dead around a year past. Claimed it was self-defence but we all knew it was nothing but downright murder. They'd just had a disagreement about a horse.'

'What about Sheriff McGiven. Didn't he take a hand?'

Bethany took her pipe out of her mouth and laughed out loud.

'Sheriff McGiven is about as good at keeping the law as Lucifer himself is about keeping law among the demons in hell. He just looks at a crime with both eyes closed and his ears shut down like a wounded mule deer.'

Sunshine couldn't quite visualize the wounded mule deer but he appreciated the symbolism.

'So what you're saying is there's no law in this town.'

'Well, if there is a law it's the law of the jungle and the king of the apes is the Cutaway brothers.'

'That makes two kings,' Sunshine said.

'I was speaking in tongues, so to say,' she replied. 'And they ain't boys, neither. They're two big ugly *hombres*, just like Slam Smith only a whole lot more ornery.'

'Maybe we should talk to them, make them see reason?' Sunshine suggested.

For the second time she took out her pipe and roared with laughter.

'You've got a hell of a lot to learn, Sunshine boy, and you better learn quick, 'cause, if you stay around here there's gonna be a deal of trouble for you.'

Sunshine considered the matter. Yes, he could just ride away and leave Bethany Bartok to her fate, whatever that might be, or he could stay at the homestead and face up to the ugly truth.

They were now within shouting distance of the homestead. Bethany clenched her pipe more tightly between her teeth.

'Aha,' she muttered. 'We've got company. Get ready for trouble, Sunshine Boy.'

Sunshine had already made up his mind to face up to the ugly truth. He held up his hand.

'Rein in the horses,' he said. 'Wait here while I go down and investigate.'

Bethany did as he said. 'You know what you're doing?' she asked.

'Not exactly,' he said. 'I just know what I have to do.'

He spurred Chingalong forward and rode down into the valley towards the homestead, where he saw two men on horseback waiting. He put his hand on the Peacemaker and eased it in its holster. *Can I use this thing?* he wondered to himself, *or am I being a damned fool? That is the big question.*

CHAPTER THREE

The two riders sat comfortably in the saddle just like they had been born there. Both had long tapering dandyish moustaches and eyes like small boot-buttons; they weren't smiling. They could have been twins except that one was a good deal heavier than the other.

Sunshine reined in a little short of them. He saw that they both had handguns on their hips.

'Did you two gentlemen want something or is this a social call?' he asked. The heavier of the two gave Sunshine a sardonic grin.

'What's that to you, yellow-hair boy?'

'I'm just enquiring on behalf of the lady of the house,' Sunshine said politely.

The other man was looking beyond Sunshine towards the buckboard where Bethany was sitting with her buffalo gun across her knees and her pipe clamped firmly between her teeth.

'Is that the lady in question?' he asked.

'No question about it,' Sunshine replied. 'That's Mrs Bethany Bartok, if you care to know.'

The larger man screwed up his eyes.

'My eyes are getting a little dim,' he said, 'but what I see is a fresh-faced maverick with a long tongue in his head.'

Sunshine smiled. 'I can't comment on that, sir, since I

can't get inside your head.'

'Well,' the smaller of the two men said, 'from where I'm setting, I see a small shrimp of a boy pretending to be a man.'

'Well, perhaps you'd be kind enough to tell this small shrimp of a man what brings you to the Bartok homestead and what you want with Mrs Bethany Bartok?'

At that moment Bethany got a little tired of waiting; she jigged her horses forward towards the homestead. She wasn't a patient woman, as Sunshine had discovered, and she wasn't used to others taking on her chores unasked. So he turned and waited as she the drove her buckboard forward.

The heavier of the two men switched his attention to her immediately as though Sunshine was nothing but a badly brought-up kid.

'You Mrs Bethany Bartok?' he shouted.

'That's my name. Who wants to know?' she asked from the corner of her mouth.

'Me and my buddy bring news,' the big *hombre* said.

'Who from?' she asked suspiciously. The lighter *hombre* spoke up:

'From your son Bart. He sends you his best wishes and hopes you're doing real well in the homestead.'

Bethany looked them over with deeply suspicious eyes.

'So Bart sent you here?'

'Let's just say we come on his behalf,' the lighter man said.

Sunshine thought that was a somewhat strange response. He glanced at Bethany and saw she was nodding judiciously.

'So where is Bart Junior right now?' she asked. The heavier man stirred himself.

'Like we said, he sends his regards.'

'But he's a little reluctant to say where he is right now,' the lighter man added. 'Just like that guy in the Good Book, he's a little nervous about coming home. But he asked us to say he's fit and well and hopes to see you soon.'

Sunshine glanced at Bethany again and saw that her jaw had tightened on that stubby pipe of hers. It was, indeed, like a weather gauge. Sunshine could guess what she was thinking from the way she gripped it with her teeth.

'So, he's not too far away from here but he's reluctant to come himself?' she speculated.

'You've summed up the position very well, Mrs Bartok,' the lighter man said with a smile. Sunshine had seen a multitude of smiles in his life and had learned to put them into three categories. There was the open-hearted, genuine smile; there was the false grin, and there was the downright sinister sneer on the face of a deceiver. He put the lighter man's smile somewhere between the second and third categories.

'Well,' Bethany said after a moment, 'if you two gents have a message from my boy, Bart Junior, you'd better get down off your horses and come right inside.'

'That's real kind of you, ma'am,' the heavier man said. Was he relieved or triumphant? Sunshine couldn't be sure.

The two *hombre* dismounted and ambled into the cabin like they owned the place. There was nothing modest about them. They just looked around with their shoe-button eyes and nodded to one another.

'Real nice place you got here,' the bigger man said.

'I got no complaint on that score,' Bethany said. 'You boys set yourselves down and I'll give you a pint of my home brew.'

'That sounds real welcome,' the lighter man said with that rather sinister grin.

The two men sat down at the table; Bethany drew off

the home brew and passed it across to them.

'Thank you, ma'am,' the heavier man said, blowing the froth off his beer and holding it up to the light. 'So you brew this up yourself?'

'Just one of my country skills,' she acknowledged. The lighter man gave Sunshine a close scrutiny.

'Are you the hired man?' he asked.

Sunshine cocked his eye and smiled; he hoped the smile looked genuine.

'I guess I've just fallen out of the sky, mister.'

'Like the good angel. . . .' the man said, 'or would it be the one they cast down into hell at the beginning of time?'

Sunshine was still smiling.

'I think you have Lucifer in mind. Depends on your point of view.' He glanced at Bethany.

'He's just about as good as he looks,' she said, with one eye half-closed.

'Sure knows how to smile, don't he?' The heavier man laughed and it sounded like he had a stone lodged in his gullet, which, Sunshine thought, was another bad sign.

Bethany had removed her pipe and balanced it on a small pot, which was obviously where it belonged when it wasn't in her mouth.

'So,' she said, looking at the lighter man, 'what do you two gents want?'

The lighter man didn't bat an eyelid.

'My, this home brew is real good,' he said. 'Could knock a man right off his feet at twenty paces.'

'Is that the answer to my question?' Bethany asked.

'Not exactly,' the lighter man said, squeezing a drop of beer from his long droopy moustache. 'That ain't the answer, ma'am. The answer is: your son Bart asked us to tell you he's a little short of ready cash at the moment.'

'You mean he hasn't got a bean?' she asked directly.

The man looked momentarily puzzled.

'Well, I wouldn't say it's quite as bad as that, ma'am. He's just a little financially embarrassed. . . .'

'Since he can't pay his way,' the heavier man added.

'So you see, he asked us to come and ask you for a certain sum to tide him over.'

'What sort of sum?' she asked. The lighter man drew in a breath.

'Shall we say a thousand dollars?'

A menacing silence fell on the room. Then the heavier man drained his mug and put it on the table.

'That's real good liquor, ma'am,' he said. Bethany fixed her eyes on the lighter man.

'So my son, Bart Junior, has sent you here to the homestead to ask for a thousand dollars. Is that what you're saying?'

The lighter man opened his hands in a fatalistic gesture.

'Sorry to bring bad tidings but that's the way it is, ma'am.'

Bethany nodded several times.

'Two questions,' she said. 'If Bart needs money so bad why didn't he come himself? And, since he was too embarrassed, like you said, how can I be sure he sent you?'

'Oh, I can put your mind at rest on that score, ma'am.' He reached into his pocket and pulled out a gold watch and chain. Then he dangled the watch in front of her and placed it on the table. 'I think you'll find that belongs to your son Bart, ma'am, or am I wrong?' Now he was grinning again in his familiar sinister fashion.

Sunshine wasn't smiling. He just felt the urge to give the man a chop to the throat.

Bethany reached out for the gold watch and weighed it in her hand. Then she turned it over and read the inscription on the back.

'Where did you get this?' she asked.

'Let's just say, your son Bart lent it to us since he needs the greenbacks.'

'So the best thing you can do is peel out the money,' the heavier man added.

Bethany was staring hard at the gold watch as though it might give her a clue to her son's whereabouts. Sunshine could see that it meant a lot to her. She turned over the watch and weighed it in her hand.

'That's a fine watch, ma'am,' the heavier man said. 'Must be worth a mint of money.'

Bethany didn't reply, but Sunshine saw her jaw muscles tighten.

'Oh, by the way, ma'am, your son Bart sent a short note so you'd know what we said came from the top of the pack.' The lighter man fished in the pocket of his vest and handed over a sliver of paper.

Bethany took the paper and read the few short sentences scrawled on it:

Hi Ma, I hope you're doing well. I'm a little tied up at the moment. So I hope you'll shell out the dollars to these two men. Your loving son, Bartholomew.

Bethany put the paper on the table next to the watch.

'Well, it's good of you to come, gentlemen,' she said calmly, 'but I have a problem here – two, in fact. First, I don't have the dollars you say my son Bart needs. The other thing is: I think I have to see him before I can hand over the money.'

'Well, that sounds reasonable, ma'am,' the lighter man said, taking up the gold watch and stowing it away in his pocket. 'So, we'll leave you to think on matters. . . .'

'But don't be too long thinking,' the heavier man said, 'because your son Bartholomew isn't feeling too well at the moment and we might not be looking after him for too long. It comes out rather expensive, you know, and we don't have too many dollars at the moment.'

The two men got up from the table just like they were mind-reading twins.

'We'll be rolling along now,' the heavier man said with false good humour.

'We'll leave you to think on things, ma'am,' the lighter man said with that hideous grin. They ambled over to the door and turned.

'Thanks again for that fine home brew,' the heavier man said.

'Think things over,' the lighter man added. 'Think things over for Bartholomew's sake, Mrs Bartok.'

'We'll be in touch,' the heavier man said.

Sunshine watched as the two men rode away. Were they going towards Logan or to some place else? It was impossible to say. When he turned back he saw that Bethany Bartok was sitting at the table with her head in her hands, but she wasn't smoking her pipe and she wasn't shedding tears. She just sat there, grim-faced and thoughtful.

'What do you figure on this?' she asked Sunshine, straight out.

'What I figure is your son has been kidnapped,' Sunshine said; he wasn't smiling. Bethany looked at him out of her eagle-bright eyes.

'Listen, Mr Shining, before the day before yesterday I didn't know you. You just rolled in like the good angel and shot up those gunmen. I need to know something.'

Sunshine sat down at the table across from her and rested his elbows on the pine surface.

'Anything you want to know just ask away,' he said.

She nodded. 'What I need to know is: are you a friend,

a genuine copper-bottomed friend?'

'Well, I don't know about the bottom part, copper or lead, but yes I'm a friend. I know I just blew in like a leaf from Missouri, but now I'm here I mean to stay. Does that answer the question?'

She nodded. 'Like I said, I can't offer you hardly anything at all, but I think I can do with your help in this.'

'In that case, I think I must put a few old cans on the corral fence and practise with that Colt revolver you lent me, because I have a strong suspicion I shall need to sharpen up my shooting skills.'

'What did you make of those two scumbags?' she asked.

'Well, you just about summed it up in one word,' he said. 'Those two smooth-tongued bags of scum wouldn't think twice about gouging out a man's eyes or shooting him in the back if the money was good enough.'

She nodded grimly. 'We agree on that. So I'm real worried about Bart.' She picked up the note. 'But one thing I am sure of. . . .'

'What's that, Mrs Bartok?'

She tapped the paper with her index finger.

'My son Bart didn't write this and he didn't sign it.' She held up the paper. 'And lookee here, what he's written.' She squinted at the paper through her small pebble spectacles. ' "I'm somewhat tied up at the moment",' she read out. 'Doesn't that tell us something?'

'Could mean he's too busy being a prisoner,' Sunshine speculated.

'That's what I think,' Bethany agreed. 'But what is more important is that he's not Bartholomew and never has been. He's Bart and that's all he ever was.'

Sunshine took the paper and studied it carefully. It smelled like it had been in close contact with strong tobacco, but that didn't mean anything since it had been in the lighter man's pocket.

'So you say this isn't your son's handwriting?'

She shook her head.

'That's no more Bart's writing than my cat's or the writing on Belshazzar's wall.'

'But you haven't got a cat,' he said. She looked at him keenly.

'And I ain't seen no writing the on the wall neither. That's exactly what I mean.'

Sunshine thought for a moment.

'Do you have a likeness of some kind, a photograph maybe?'

'Yes, I do.' She got up from the table and went over to a ramshackle sideboard from which she picked up a photo in a somewhat elaborate frame. She brought it back to the table and stood it in front of Sunshine. 'This was taken some five years back, just before my man Bart Senior took bad and died. I don't see it helps us much.'

Sunshine shook his head.

'I'm not sure about that. At least it helps me to focus in on your son Bart.' He took the frame in his hands and held it close. It showed just an ordinary family dressed in the manner of the day. Hard-working people who used all their strength and energy to keep the wolf from the door. The father didn't look exactly sick but, at the same time, he didn't look to be in the best of health either. The boy, Bart Junior, couldn't have been more than sixteen and the girl, Elspeth, was even younger. She had the eagle eyes of her mother and looked anxious to explore the world.

To Sunshine it was a sad picture, the picture of a family that didn't know that break-up was just around the corner. Even Bethany looked somehow different, a little more hopeful about life in general.

'What do you see?' Bethany asked him.

'I see an ordinary family with hopes for the future,' he said. 'What happened to those two kids?'

'Well, after their pa died a family from the East took Elspeth under their wing. They could see she was bright and eager and they offered to have her educated at their expense.' She shrugged. 'As for Bart, he just lit out after his pa died. He sort of idealized Bart Senior and went to pieces after he died. There weren't nothing I could do to stop him. My guess is he got in with a bad bunch and this is the result.'

Sunshine placed the framed photo respectfully on the table.

'That's a real nice picture, ma'am, and it has convinced me I'm doing the right thing.'

'Well, I'm glad about that, Sunshine, because to tell you the truth, I feel real sick to my stomach about this whole business. So what do we do next?'

Sunshine worked his jaw for a moment.

'Could there be some sort of tie-up between these two moustachioed gents and the Cutaway brothers, d'you think?'

'I've thought about that,' she said. Then she took up her pipe and started loading it with tobacco. Sunshine got up from the table, then sat down again.

'Do you happened to have a pen and ink, Bethany?'

'I sure do,' she said. 'You thinking of writing a letter or something?'

'In this case it's something,' he said. 'What I'm going to do is draw portraits of those two kidnappers so I remember exactly what they look like.'

'Well, that's a good idea if you can draw as good as you talk,' she said. Then she produced pen and paper and Sunshine set himself to drawing the two *hombres*. Bethany got up from the table.

'There's chores to do. I got to feed the livestock and look around the place, see everything's in good order. You don't have too much rest in a place like this.'

While she was out Sunshine concentrated on the portraits till he had the two faces just about right. While he wasn't exactly proud of them he thought they were good likenesses. When Bethany came in, she said:

'Someone's been poking around the place.'

'You seen the signs?'

Bethany sniffed. 'The animals notice these things. Even that hoss of yours seemed a little restless.'

'Well, that's not surprising since Chingalong likes to keep on the move.'

She looked down at the portraits on the table.

'My, my,' she said. 'These are just the living image of those two rascals, just like they're all set to talk to a person.'

'That's good,' said Sunshine, 'because I hope you're going to talk to me and tell me a whole lot more than I know right now.'

'Did you study art work at school?' she asked.

'To tell you the truth, I didn't study much at all,' he admitted. 'I just like observing nature. Those two moustachioed gents were two of nature's great monstrosities.'

'So, what do you aim to do with those portraits?'

'Well, with your permission, Mrs Bartok, tomorrow come sunup I'm going to ride into town and see what I can dig up.'

She eyed him cautiously.

'You don't need my permission, son. You just need a word of advice.'

'And what would that be?' he asked.

'Strap that gunbelt to your side and be ready to use that hogleg if necessary because town can be more than a little rough at times, as you saw earlier, and you got to be ready.'

'I'll bear that in mind,' he said.

'And don't come back dead,' she said, 'because dead you won't be no good to me at all.'

CHAPTER FOUR

Next morning they were both up good and early. Bethany served a full breakfast that included almost everything she could devise.

'So you're set on going into town?' she said.

'I'm set to go into Logan,' he agreed. 'I don't know what I'll find but I have a hunch I'll find something.' He went out and saddled up.

'We're going right into town, buddy,' he told Chingalong. 'You do right and we'll get along just fine.'

They trotted along nice and easy and it didn't seem far at all. They went past the store with the horse trough outside, then right through to the end of town. There wasn't much doing and not many people around. So they turned and went back until they came to the sign that said CLOSE SHAVE and underneath *We do you good.*

'OK, buddy, this is the spot,' Sunshine said to the horse. He dismounted and tied Chingalong to the hitching rail. 'Just in case you're tempted to take a stroll,' he added.

He walked into the barber shop and saw a man sitting in a chair facing the door. He had practically no hair on his head at all.

'Are you the receptionist?' Sunshine asked him.

'No, I'm the barber and the funeral director,' the man

replied. 'Which service would you prefer?'

'If there's a choice, I think I'll go for the barber. Right now I think I need a haircut.'

The barber gave him a critical look.

'Pity to spoil such a good head of hair. How did you get it so yellow? Did it come naturally or did you dunk it in a vat of dye?'

'That's just the way it sprouted out,' Sunshine said, 'so I've decided to keep it that way till I grow old and grey.'

The barber studied him critically again.

'How do you want it?' he asked.

'Well, I don't want to come out bald if that's what you mean. Just trim it back by two or three inches so I look a little more hand in hat.'

'I think I might manage that,' the barber said. 'Why don't you just sit yourself down in the chair and make yourself good and comfortable.' The barber chuckled as he draped a big cloth over Sunshine's front. 'So you're keeping that gunboat on?' he said.

'That seems the best policy,' Sunshine conceded. The barber didn't argue with that.

'I heard what happened the other day,' he said.

'What did happen?' Sunshine asked.

The barber started snipping and combing, laughing quietly to himself.

'Like you came into town with that half-crazy woman Beth Bartok.'

'Well, sure I came into town with her,' Sunshine agreed, 'but I have to disagree with you on one thing. Bethany Bartok isn't even a quarter crazy. She has a lot going for her – and enough cojones for two men.'

The barber stopped snipping.

'You're right about that. Mrs Bartok is as brave as any turkey-cock I know.' The barber snipped the air for a moment. 'And another thing: I saw what you did to that gunslinger Slam Smith. I saw him trying to pull himself out of the water trough and you pushing him right down again, I won't forget that in a thousand years.'

'Well, I hope you come from a long-lived family,' Sunshine said.

The barber held a mirror up so Sunshine could see what the scissors had accomplished.

'How's that, sir?'

Sunshine could see he'd done a presentable job. His hair had shrunk but his face and head looked a whole lot bigger. The barber untied the cloth and took it to the door, where he shook the clippings on to the sidewalk.

'Good for the birds,' he said to himself, 'except they might not like their nests looking quite so bright.' He chuckled as he came into the shop again. 'Will there be anything else, good sir?'

Sunshine showed him the two drawings.

'Take a look at these pictures and tell me what you see.'

The barber took the two portraits and held them up to the light.

'My my, my good sir. So you're an artist too?'

'I just do a few sketches from time to time. The question is, have you seen these two moustachioed gents anywhere around?'

'Sure I've seen them. You've got them just about right.'

'That's good because I need to talk to them.'

The barber grinned.

'They ain't much for talking – at least, not from their mouths. They generally talk more with their shooters.'

'That's what I suspected, and that's why I need to talk to them. So maybe you can tell me who they are and where I can find them?'

The barber pulled his face into a frown.

'Well, young sir, you're new to this town and I think you have a lot to learn.'

'Like what in particular?' Sunshine asked.

'Like it ain't healthy to ask too many questions around here.'

'Not even when people's lives are at risk?' Sunshine said.

The barber was still frowning, only now he looked more like a funeral director than a barber.

'Whose lives?' he asked guardedly.

Sunshine crammed his hat on his head. It fitted just fine.

'Like the life of Bart Bartok Junior,' he suggested. The barber's eyes widened somewhat.

'You mean Mrs Bethany Bartok's son?'

'So you remember the boy?' Sunshine said. The barber looked at the door and shook his head.

'Why, what happened to Bart Junior?' he asked.

'Nothing so far,' said Sunshine, 'but I have reason to believe he's been kidnapped.' He waited for this to sink in. 'And he's being held by those two moustachioed gents – or by someone who's using them as a front.'

'What makes you think that?'

Sunshine saw little beads of sweat on the barber's bald pate. He nodded.

'I'm gonna tell you what happened yesterday.'

The barber set himself down on a chair while Sunshine told him about the events of the day before, including the ransom demand. The barber sat there like a stone image until Sunshine came to the ransom demand. Then the barber, looking shocked, grunted and shook his head.

'I can't believe this,' he said. 'So you think that boy's life is in danger?'

'I do believe it might be,' Sunshine told him. 'So maybe

you can help me on this?'

'How can I help?' Now larger beads of sweat were breaking out all over the barber's forehead.

'Well, I have to find out where that boy's being held,' Sunshine said.

'That won't be easy. He could be anywhere.'

'The point is, he must be somewhere.' Sunshine swivelled his chair round to face the barber. 'Now, mister, there is something else you can help me with, too. Is there a tie-up between those two scarmouches and the Cutaway brothers?'

The barber's jaw dropped, but what he might have said next remained a mystery because at that moment the door of the shop swung open to reveal a burly man in a wide-brimmed Stetson. He didn't look any too friendly.

The barber gave a sort of squawk, sounding like a chicken that sees the chicken farmer coming towards it with a sharp knife.

'Why, good morning, Mr Smith,' he croaked. The new arrival was Slam Smith, the man whom Sunshine had dunked in the drinking trough the day before.

The man stood in the doorway and peered down at Sunshine through bloodshot, malevolent eyes, looking like the Devil incarnate.

'So you're back in town,' he snarled through tobacco-stained whiskers. Sunshine swung round in the chair.

'Thought I'd ride in for a hair trim,' he said, sounding calmer than he felt. He was glad to be sitting down because he thought his legs might turn to jelly if he tried to get up, and it gave him a moment longer to get used to what might be about to happen.

'You cut this cissy-boy's hair?' the bully barked at the barber.

The barber tried to reply but his mouth was suddenly too dry and nothing came out. Slam Smith's grin widened and he switched to Sunshine again.

'I see you got your gunbelt strapped on today, sonny. You think you can use that toy or is it just to impress your *amigos?*'

Sunshine suddenly felt anger welling up.

'I guess I won't know the answer to that question until the time comes,' he said. Slam Smith sniggered.

'Well, the time's come a little sooner than you expected, sonny boy. Why don't you just step outside on to Main Street and we'll see what you can do with that toy.'

Sunshine glanced at the barber and the barber gave a slight shake of his head. Sunshine dragged himself up from the chair and found, to his surprise, that his legs were far less shaky than he had feared. *Is this the end or the beginning?* he asked himself. He reached down to check that the Colt Peacemaker was in place; when he looked up again he was looking at the barrel of a gun. Slam Smith chuckled.

'Don't try anything in here, sonny boy. After all, we don't want to spill your blood all over the floor, do we?'

'What exactly do you want?' Sunshine asked him.

'What I want is for you count to three and then come out on to Main Street and we'll take it from there.' Smith backed out through the door and walked across the sidewalk on to the dust of Main Street.

Sunshine turned to the barber, who looked more like a stone statue than a man, except that he was trembling.

'What do I do now?' Sunshine asked him.

'Well, you have a choice,' the barber said. 'Either you can go out on to Main Street and face up to that bully and his shooter, or you can disappear through the shop and vamoose out through the back way.'

Sunshine thought things over. The second option was certainly tempting. He could run and live to fight another day. On the other hand vamoosing had its down side: if he ran he would be branded a coward and become a laughing-stock and that wouldn't help anyone, least of all him.

'Did you notice something?' he asked the barber.

'Nothing in particular,' the barber admitted, 'except Slam Smith was mad enough to kill a man.'

'He sure was mad,' Sunshine admitted, 'but he was also drunk as a skunk. The way he walked across the sidewalk and the way he stank of booze. Does he always sway and stink like that?'

'Slam Slam is drunk but that's nothing unusual. He spends most of his time tipping back the bottle and when he's sober he's usually snoring away in some cathouse.'

Sunshine shook his head. 'Well then, that means he's a really sad case and I'm sorry for him.'

'Don't waste your tears, because he sure won't be sorry when he shoots you down, son.'

Sunshine braced himself. 'I've made up my mind. I'm going out to face the music, whatever tune it might play.'

The barber shook his head. 'Well, I prefer a dance to a funeral march and I hope you can do a jig, 'cause I hear there's a deal of dancing and rejoicing in heaven.'

'Thanks for the encouraging words,' Sunshine said.

He stepped out on to the sidewalk. For some unfathomable reason his legs weren't shaking at all. The bully Slam Smith was standing no more than a hundred feet away with his back to the sun. He had his legs apart and his hands by his sides and he looked as steady as Pike's Peak.

'You said your prayers, sonny boy?' he snarled.

'You got your dancing shoes ready?' Sunshine shouted back. 'They tell me they dance all day in hell but the dances are sort of grotesque.'

The word *grotesque* had a strange effect on the bully, as if an invisible bullet had struck him right in the middle of the forehead.

Don't weaken and don't feel sorry for him, Sunshine told himself. *Just keep talking and using words as bullets.*

'Mr Smith,' he said, 'why don't you just walk into the saloon, have a pint of good booze, then lie down somewhere and take a long nap?'

That hit Slam Smith just like a second bullet between the eyes. His head jerked back.

'You think I'm too pissed-up to kill you, boy?' he roared.

'I think you're too pissed-up not to try,' Sunshine replied.

Slam Smith turned purple in the face and his eyes flamed with fury.

'Get you to hell!' he raged. He reached down for his shooter and tried to pull it free. He wasn't a quick-draw man and he never would be, especially when he was drunk, which was most of the time.

Sunshine saw what was coming; he dodged back into the shadows of the overhang, drew the Peacemaker and fired. Slam Smith's shot had come a split second later; the bullet went wide, smashing a window in the barber shop. Sunshine had aimed low but the bullet had found its mark. Smith staggered back and fell.

Sunshine walked forward under the overhang and stepped out on to Main Street. Slam Smith was struggling to get to his feet but it was too difficult since Sunshine's bullet had struck his right leg just below the knee, shattering the bone; blood was spurting from the wound on to the dust of the street. Smith raised his shooter and tried to level it but the pain from his wound defeated him; he groaned and hopped to one side.

Sunshine levelled the Peacemaker and drew back the hammer.

'Just drop that gun before I shoot you right between the eyes,' he said.

Slam Smith half-rose, then fell back, clutching his wounded leg. His shooter fell into the dust of Main Street. He stared at Sunshine in total bewilderment and terror, as though he was seeing a railway locomotive coming full tilt towards him.

Sunshine drew back, still holding the Peacemaker.

'Somebody get help to this man before he bleeds to death,' he shouted. Now his legs were beginning to feel like jelly, after all.

'Send for the sawbones,' the barber shouted. He had just emerged from the shop with his first-aid kit. 'Lie down right there,' he said to Smith. 'I'm gonna tie that wound so you don't lose too much blood.'

He cut back Smith's pants so that the wound was revealed. Then he tied it up good and tight to stanch the bleeding. Smith groaned and passed out.

'That was good shooting,' a man said.

Sunshine shook his head. He felt sort of dazed and ready to fall. So he sat down on the sidewalk step and looked at the Peacemaker. *Did I really shoot that man in the leg or was I dreaming?* he wondered to himself. It was as though he had watched someone who wasn't quite him firing the shot. He looked up and saw a well-dressed dandyish man with a well-groomed beard, wearing a tall black hat.

'Was that your first time, young man?' the stranger asked.

'First time for what?' Sunshine asked in a daze.

'The first time you shot someone?' the man asked with a benign smile. Sunshine shook his head.

'Well, I don't make a habit of it.'

'Good at talking, too. That's always useful in a man, especially out here in the wilderness where most men have only four words to their name.'

'What would they be, sir?'

The man shrugged and smiled. 'They would be "yes", "no", and "can't remember".'

The barber was still tending Slam Smith, who lay groaning on the sidewalk; the barber sure knew what he was doing. He had that leg bound up so professionally he might have been the doc himself.

'Will he live?' Sunshine asked. The man in the tall hat looked quizzical.

'Oh, he'll most probably live but he'll be short of a leg for the rest of his life.'

He turned to address the small crowd that had gathered. 'Will someone walk over to the saloon and order a stiff pull of whiskey for the wounded man. I can't abide to see a man suffer like this.'

'Yes, Mr Cutaway,' someone said. The eyes under the tall black hat looked down at Sunshine.

'I'm Jacob Cutaway,' he said. 'My friends call me Jed and everyone else calls me Mr Cutaway.'

'I'm right glad to meet you, Mr Cutaway,' Sunshine replied. Jacob Cutaway shook his head slowly.

'You look sort of stressed out, young man,' he said. 'Why don't you step across to the saloon and have a drink at my expense?'

'Thank you, Mr Cutaway. I believe I will . . . no strings attached?'

The tall man laughed. 'We don't have strings here, Mr . . . what did you say your name was?'

'Stubbs Shining,' Sunshine said. 'People call me Sunshine because I look a little young for my age.'

'Well, I should say you acted like a man today,' Jed Cutaway said.

They walked across Main Street and into the Big Nugget saloon, where everyone doffed his hat to Jed Cutaway and called him 'sir' or 'Mr Cutaway'.

'I want a big whiskey for this young man – and make it the best; I don't want any of that hooch you serve up for most of your customers.'

The man behind the bar smiled ingratiatingly.

'Of course, Mr Cutaway, only the best for you and your friends.'

Jed Cutaway nodded. 'And serve up a good juicy steak for this young man, because he's earned it.'

'Very good, Mr Cutaway,' the barman said, somewhat over-enthusiastically.

A sip or two of that good strong whiskey and Sunshine felt a deal better. When the steak arrived he thought it must be the juiciest in the world. Jed Cutaway sat across from him and nodded sagely.

'Yes, you do look kind of young,' he observed. 'Where do you come from?'

'Back East,' Sunshine told him. 'Missouri.'

'Well, they obviously don't have steaks like this in Missouri.'

Sunshine didn't bother to contradict him; he was too busy chewing his steak and thinking.

'I heard how you dunked Slam Smith in the water trough,' Jed Cutaway said. 'That was quite a feat considering he must be twice your weight.'

'I was just lucky,' Sunshine admitted modestly. 'He

51

more or less tipped himself over.'

Jed Cutaway stroked his beard thoughtfully. He obviously enjoyed preening himself.

'Are you looking for work, young man?' he asked. Sunshine shook his head.

'Right now I'm helping out at a farmstead close by.'

Jed Cutaway narrowed his eyes. 'Is that a fact. Is the pay good?'

Sunshine looked up and smiled. 'I don't know. I haven't been paid yet.'

Jed Cutaway gave a benign chuckle.

'I guess you must be working for that slightly whacky lady, Beth Bartok.'

'I'm not too familiar with that word "whacky",' Sunshine said. 'I would say she's more gritty than whacky. She's mired in a whole lot of difficulties at the moment and she's fighting bravely to try to get out of that pile of horse shit.'

Jed Cutaway shook his head and grinned.

'So the young man from the East rides in like a knight in shining armour to redress the balance,' he said.

'I haven't read too many of the classics, so I can't comment on that,' Sunshine replied. He wondered whether he should finish his steak, then decided he probably should, so he stabbed a large chunk of meat, stuck it in his mouth and started chewing again. Jed Cutaway looked thoughtful.

'She can't win, you know,' he said. 'I've offered to help her out.'

'You mean by sending your men to shoot out her windows?' Sunshine said through his mouthful of steak. Jed Cutaway tilted his head to one side for a moment.

'The difficulty is, things get a little out of hand from time to time.'

Sunshine took time to finish his steak; he then concentrated on the good rye whiskey. Jed Cutaway ran his hand lovingly through his beard again.

'I guess it was you who shot up Brad Bassington and the boys the other day,' he remarked.

Sunshine looked about for something to wipe his mouth on and a waiter rushed up to offer him a kerchief.

'I wouldn't say I shot them up. I just fired a couple of shots over their heads to discourage them,' he corrected. Jed Cutaway gave a melodious chuckle.

'Why did you do that, Mr Shining?'

Sunshine nodded in agreement with himself.

'I guess I thought it was a little unfair, four gunmen gunning down on a little old lady and shooting out her windows like that. So I acted on the spur of the moment.'

Jed Cutaway was still chuckling.

'That "little old lady" has a good line in buffalo guns,' he said, 'and she's not so old, anyway.'

'She cooks up a really good stew,' Sunshine told him. He swigged back the last of the whiskey and placed his glass on the table. The waiter, standing at the ready by the bar, rushed up to replenish it but Sunshine covered it with his hand. The waiter backed away, bowing to Jed Cutaway who ignored him.

'Listen, Mr Shining,' Cutaway said to Sunshine, 'I have a proposition to put on the table.'

Sunshine gave him one of his best smiles. 'I'm listening with both ears, Mr Cutaway.'

'If you come and work for me I'll make it worth your while.'

'In what way would that be, Mr Cutaway?'

Jed Cutaway took a moment or two to reply. Then he said:

'Well, I'd pay you top dollar and give you a place to live;

53

that means a lot in these parts.'

It sounded quite generous in the circumstances.

'And what would I do?' Sunshine asked him. 'Like . . . shooting out the windows of old ladies?'

Jed Cutaway smiled. It was as though nothing threw him off balance.

'That was a mistake and those boys will pay for it. In fact, Slam Smith already has. You've got more than an ounce of brain, Mr Shining, and a good tongue in your head. That's what I like about you. You could have a great future before you, you know that?' He sounded quite persuasive. Sunshine continued smiling.

'That all seems generous, Mr Cutaway, and I'll turn your offer over in my head.'

'You do that, Mr Shining.' Jed Cutaway stretched out his hand towards Sunshine but Sunshine didn't take it. He looked Jed Cutaway right in the eye.

'I have two questions for you, Mr Cutaway.'

Jed Cutaway stared right back.

'Well, questions need answers, so fire away, Mr Shining.'

Sunshine nodded but his eyes had narrowed.

'The first question is, why do you want Bethany Bartok's farm so badly? The second is this: where are those two moustachioed gents holding Bart Bartok?'

Jed Cutaway didn't shift his gaze.

'What do you mean: "holding Bart Bartok"?'

Sunshine saw immediately that Cutaway was either a very good actor or that he was genuinely surprised. So he took out his sketches of the two moustachioed gents and laid them on the table.

'It seems that Bart Bartok, Bethany Bartok's son, has been kidnapped. These two gents came to the farmstead yesterday and told Mrs Bartok they'd come on Bart's behalf; they asked for one thousand dollars.'

Sunshine watched as Jed Cutaway took up the sketches and peered at them thoughtfully.

'You know these two gents, Mr Cutaway?' he asked. Jed Cutaway nodded slowly.

'These are good likenesses,' he said, 'and I do know these two *hombres*.' Sunshine gave an inward sigh of relief.

'Well, these two *hombre* are holding Bart Bartok – or they're working for someone who is. Either way, it doesn't look good for Mrs Bartok and her son Bart. So I'm wondering what you can do to help me.' He peered at Jed Cutaway so intently that Cutaway momentarily averted his gaze.

'I'll need to think on this, Mr Shining,' he said after a moment.

'I'm sure Mrs Bartok will be greatly obliged if you do.'

CHAPTER FIVE

It was well nigh sundown before Sunshine got back to the Bartok spread. Bethany Bartok was tending the stock and she shaded her eyes from the declining sun as he approached.

'You've been an awful long time,' she said. 'I was beginning to think you'd jumped ship and ridden off some place else.'

'I've been busy as a beaver,' he replied, 'but I haven't been building a dam. I've been taking a haircut and talking to Jed Cutaway.'

Despite her fatalistic nature, Bethany Bartok raised her eyebrows in amazement.

'You talked to Jed Cutaway?'

'He bought me a huge steak dinner and a good measure of honest rye whiskey.'

'Well, miracles do happen,' she said, 'though I've yet to see one myself. You'd better come inside and tell me the full story,'

I'll just make sure Chingalong's happy first,' he said. 'He's had a busy day looking at the world and wondering why humankind acts so crazy. Isn't that so, Chingalong?'

Chingalong didn't bother to reply. He wasn't crazy enough to drink whiskey but liked good oats and clear water, which were probably a whole lot better for him.

*

Bethany soon had the stewpot bubbling away; it smelled like heaven had come down to earth. Then she poured out a mug of her home brew and lit her stubby pipe.

'Now,' she said, 'I don't want no fairy tales. Just tell me the whole story and be damned.'

'I can't make any promises but I hope I won't be damned any time soon. I'm not quite ready for it yet.'

Sunshine told her everything that had happened from the haircut to the shooting, then went on to tell of the feast with Jed Cutaway. She listened, nodding judiciously from time to time, her pipe clamped firmly between her teeth.

'My my,' she said, 'so you shot that bully in the leg?'

' 'Fraid so,' he said. 'That Peacemaker sure made peace between us, but the guy was really pissed up so it doesn't count for much.'

'Well, I guess it counts with Jed Cutaway if he offered you a job.' She narrowed her eyes. 'Have you a mind to take him up on the offer?'

Sunshine smiled. 'I told him I'd think on the matter.'

'You better think carefully, or you might end up as a hired killer,' she said.

'I'd have to practise my shooting a whole lot more before that could be.'

Bethany wasn't smiling; she was obviously somewhat disturbed by the idea.

'So, you think Cutaway knows those two moustachioed gorillas?' she said.

'Well, he didn't give me names, but I'm sure he knows who they are and who they operate for.'

'You mean it isn't him?'

'My impression is he has no love for those two gun-toting gorillas, which, by the way, is a little insulting to our distant relations. Those gorillas might be working for him or they might not be. It's difficult to say.'

Bethany nodded grimly. 'I ought to tell you something: those two critters showed up again today.'

'Is that so?'

She nodded. 'They showed up shortly after you left this morning.'

Sunshine tilted his head to one side. 'They probably waited for me to leave and then came down to put the frighteners on you. Which may mean that your son Bart is being held somewhere quite close to here.'

'Well, I'm worried real sick about Bart.' Her face looked quite grey and the worry lines seemed to have become more deeply ingrained.

'Tell me what happened this morning,' Sunshine said.

'They just rode down as I was milking Jess,' she said. 'They sat their horses and grinned at me – they were all smiles and good manners, like before. "Good morning, Mrs Bartok," the smaller one called out. "How you feeling today?"

'I wasn't about to tell him tell him I felt sick to my stomach, and I wasn't gonna let them see I was worried to death about Bart, was I? Then he asked me if I'd considered their offer and whether I was ready to hand over the thousand dollars to them for Bart's benefit. That's the word they used: "benefit". Then they showed me his watch again and the smaller guy said it was to prove they were genuine.'

Sunshine nodded. 'Those two moustachioes are just about as genuine as two boa constrictors.'

'Why do you keep blinding me with words?' she asked him. 'What in hell is a boa constrictor, anyway?'

'A boa constrictor is a kind of snake, but it doesn't have poisonous fangs like the rattler. It just coils round its victim and crushes it to death.'

'Well, that just about describes those two moustachioed gents.' She gave a mirthless grin. 'The big question is: how am I gonna save my son Bart from their scaly coils?'

Sunshine creased his brows. 'I've been thinking about that all the way back from town.'

'Have you come up with an answer yet?'

Sunshine shook his head. 'Not yet, but the faint outline of a thought has been forming in my mind.'

'Well, I hope that thought will come up more clearly in time to save Bart,' she said lugubriously. 'Maybe you can tell me about it before it fades out altogether.'

They sat on either side of the stove.

'The way I figure it,' Sunshine said. 'Those two scaramouches and Jed Cutaway want the same thing – and it isn't money. Money's part of it but they've got their eyes on something else: your land.'

Bethany Bartok ran her hand over the side of her face.

'Why the hell should they want a small patch of dirt in the middle of nowhere?' she asked. 'It don't make no kind of sense. Those Cutaway boys own the whole range for miles around here. Their daddy ran a big cattle ranch and they still own most of it. Why in hell's name should they want to buy me out?'

Sunshine nodded. 'That's exactly what we have to find out, Mrs Bartok.'

Sunshine had never had worries to disturb his sleep, but on this night he did turn over once or twice. The second time he woke after a vivid dream. In the dream he was riding Chingalong and Chingalong spoke like Balaam's ass.

'You think you people are a whole lot more savvy than us,' the horse said in a low horsey tone, and he was sort of grinning back at Sunshine.

Sunshine wanted to reply but he found he couldn't find the words. He was sort of tongue-tied, which was unusual for him.

'Don't bother to say anything, Sunshine,' Chingalong continued. 'Just listen to what I say and benefit from my horse sense.'

Sunshine didn't argue. Deep inside he knew he was dreaming but dreams can search very deep. Some of his best thoughts came in the night.

'Just listen and I'll tell you what to do,' Chingalong continued. 'Just give me my nose and I'll take you where you want to go.'

Sunshine wanted to ask the horse how he knew where he wanted to go but at that point he woke with a start. *What a damned fool dream!* he thought and drifted off to sleep again.

When he got himself out of bed next morning Bethany Bartok was doing her morning chores as usual. So he went out, inhaled deeply, and dunked his head under the pump. When he came up again and looked around he saw Bethany walking towards him, carrying a pail of rich, creamy milk.

'So you got your butt out of sleepyland,' she sang out.

'I sure did,' he agreed. 'That strange land has a lot of good ideas floating around in it.'

'Like what?' she asked. 'Did you see any angels or demons up there?'

'Nothing in particular,' he said. 'But I did see a talking horse by the name of Chingalong.'

She laughed. 'Well you'd best come inside and tell me what he said while you still remember it, because in my experience dreams generally fade away like the morning mist.'

They went inside together and had breakfast. It was early for Sunshine but late for Bethany since she'd been up and about for over an hour.

'You remember what Chingalong said?' she asked him.

'He said I should mount up and he'd take me some place where I would learn something important.'

'D'you take notice of such foolishness?' she asked him.

'Well, I have a theory about that. That horse is a good buddy but he doesn't say a lot, but when he speaks he likes me to take him seriously. So that's what I must do. My theory is that when a horse or some other critter speaks it's really something coming from deep inside your own mind and you have to listen.'

'That sounds plumb crazy to me. If I didn't know you better I'd think the sun had got under your hat and roasted your brain.'

'Maybe it has and maybe it hasn't. That's what I aim to find out. Do you have a map of the homestead?'

'Of course I do. I keep it somewhere in that old desk of mine. I call it a desk but it's no more than a few sticks held together with rusty nails. My man Bart planned to get something grander but I'm afraid he left it too late.'

She rummaged in the desk and brought out a map rolled up in a tube of cardboard. She unrolled it on to the table and held it down with coffee mugs.

'Is this another of your mysteries, or did that old hoss of yourn tell you about it in your sleep?' she asked him.

'No. After he said what he said I put two and two together and came up with five.' Sunshine leaned forward and studied the map. The farmstead was a lot bigger than he had supposed. 'So you own all this land,' he said, 'right down to the creek?'

'Yes, I do,' she affirmed, 'and that's what keeps me on my feet most of the day and half the night.'

He glanced at her and wondered how long she could keep going. She was tough and wiry but she wasn't getting any younger. He ran his finger across the map and down to the creek.

'What's this area here hatched in black?'

'That's what I call "the Badlands",' she said.

'Why "the Badlands?" ' he asked.

'That's because they're no good to man or beast,' she said. 'You can't graze cattle there and you can't grow corn there. That land is fit for nothing, and it bubbles up from time to time. I heard the Indians call it "Bad Medicine Pipe" 'cause it puffs out foul stinking air from time to time.'

'Is that so?' Sunshine drummed on the table with his fingers.

'What is that fanciful brain of yourn cooking up now?' she asked him.

'That's Chingalong speaking again and he's saying: "Sunshine, you have to go to that place and take a looksee".'

They went to the stable and saddled up. Bethany sat astride a bay mare; Sunshine was riding Chingalong as usual.

'Listen up,' he said to Chingalong as he threw the saddle over him and tightened the cinch. 'Whether you know it or not, I mean to follow your advice, so you'd better be right.'

Chingalong flexed back his ears but said nothing.

'I do believe that hoss knows what you're saying to him,' Bethany said.

'You can bet your last silver dollar on that,' Sunshine replied.

They rode down through the pasture and on towards the creek. There were steers in the pasture and as Sunshine and Bethany rode by they looked up in surprise before putting their heads down to graze again.

'Don't waste much time, do they?' Sunshine observed.

'They know what's good for them,' Bethany told him.

'This is a good farm,' Sunshine said, 'but you have to get real. How long d'you think you can keep going here on your own?'

Bethany clamped her teeth firmly on her pipe.

'Just as a long as it takes or until I drop down and die,' she said. 'And I'm as real as I can be and I know I need to hire hands to help me out.' She glanced at him from the corner of her eye. 'You wouldn't be interested, would you, Mr Shining?'

Sunshine wrinkled his nose. 'Well, I never thought of myself as a farmer. That's why I rode West looking for adventure.'

'Well, you've already had a good helping of that, whatever it is,' she said.

Now they came close to the creek. As they rode along Bethany pointed to the right.

'You see that belt of trees over yonder. That's where the Badlands begin.'

They rode through the trees until they came to the trees that Bethany had indicated, where they reined in their horses.

'Well, this is the place,' she said. 'No good for man or beast.'

Sunshine looked out over the desolate land and a shudder went through his spine. What he saw was like a wilderness, where little would grow and no animal could graze. It was a relatively small area and certainly no good for farming, but here and there Sunshine saw pits from which steam rose and bubbles popped on the surface.

'I think I know why Chingalong led me here in my dreams,' he said.

Chingalong's ears twitched back but as usual he said nothing.

'Well, what did that crazy hoss say to you?' Bethany asked him.

Sunshine shook his head. 'He said tell that good lady you've struck oil or gas – or maybe both.'

Bethany took her pipe out of her mouth and stared at him in amazement.

'Are you sure about that?'

'Somebody's sure,' he said. 'That's why those Cutaways want to get their hands on the property; it might be why your son Bart has been kidnapped, too.'

'Well, I'll be danged!' she said. 'How in the devil's name can that be?'

'Why, lookee here,' she said a moment later. Sunshine saw two riders riding towards them, skirting round the Badlands. Even from where he sat Sunshine could recognize one as Jed Cutaway. The two riders appeared to be alone.

'What do we do now?' Bethany asked him.

'What we do is we keep ourselves calm and wait,' Sunshine advised.

So they sat their horses and waited. Bethany Bartok wasn't a patient woman but she stuck her pipe in her mouth and gritted her teeth.

The two riders rode forward until they were within talking distance; then they reined in.

'Good morrow, dear lady,' Jed Cutaway said, raising his tall black hat. 'Good morrow, Mr Shining.' He indicated his companion. 'I don't think you've met my brother, Mr Shining.'

'I've heard about him,' Sunshine said politely. 'Good morning, Mr Cutaway.'

The second brother doffed his Stetson. 'The name's James. It's a pleasure to meet you, Mr Shining.'

'My pleasure too, Mr Cutaway.'

'I heard about your exploits in town yesterday,' James Cutaway replied.

'That was nothing,' Sunshine said. 'I was just sorry I had to shoot that man in the leg.'

'Could have been the head.' James Cutaway grinned.

Jed Cutaway chuckled. 'We were hoping to see you, Mrs Bartok. There's something we wanted to talk to you about.'

'A proposition,' James Cutaway added. 'It concerns your son Bart.'

Sunshine glanced at Bethany and saw her wince.

'What's the proposition?' she asked suspiciously.

Both brothers were smiling and Sunshine was trying to work out how genuine their smiles were.

'Why don't you come up to the cabin and you can put your proposition to me?' Bethany suggested. The two brothers exchanged smiles.

'Why don't we do that?' Jed Cutaway said.

Sunshine observed that the brothers took note of every detail as they rode towards the cluster of buildings that constituted what Bethany Bartok called the homestead.

'How many head of cattle do you run here, Mrs Bartok?' James Cutaway asked.

'A few,' she replied noncommittally.

'It must be real hard managing the spread on your own,' he suggested.

'I manage,' she replied, giving Sunshine a wary glance.

'You know, one time our pa and his brother ran cattle on the whole of this range,' James Cutaway said. 'You looked out every which way right to the mountains and our cattle grazed as far as the eye could see.'

'So I hear,' Bethany said, 'but the way I look at it, things change, Mr Cutaway. Things change and we have to change with them.'

'That's the truth, Mrs Bartok,' Jed Cutaway said. 'You have a wise head on your shoulders, dear lady.'

Sunshine had been studying the two brothers and he'd noticed the differences between them. James was more hard-edged than his brother and Jed was more of a flatterer and a diplomat. Sunshine wondered whether they were as brotherly as they pretended to be.

When they reached Bethany's cabin she dismounted.

'Set yourselves down on the porch, gentlemen,' she said. 'Maybe Mr Shining will be good enough to feed and water the horses and I'll bring you something to wash away the dust from your throats.'

'Thank you kindly, ma'am,' Jed Cutaway said.

Sunshine took the horses to the drinking trough. When he came back Bethany was serving tankards of her home brew to the brothers.

'This your own brew, Mrs Bartok?' Jed Cutaway asked her.

'This is my brew,' she affirmed. 'Usually it comes out good and strong.'

'Tastes kind of cheesy,' James Cutaway said. 'But it's wholesome and good.'

They sat for a time drinking the beer.

'What's the proposition?' Bethany asked abruptly. The brothers exchanged glances.

'Well, now, Mrs Bartok,' Jed said, 'we've been thinking some on your son Bart and the fact that he's being held captive.'

'Kidnapped's the word,' James put in.

'And we want to help you find him and punish those who are holding him.'

Bethany's lip trembled but she held her nerve.

'That's good news, Mr Cutaway, but tell me how you can do that?'

There was a momentary pause, as though the brothers

didn't know which of them should continue. Then James spoke up again.

'Well, Mrs Bartok, we hear most of what's going on in this territory and we know who those two visiting gents are.'

'That's because they used to work for us,' Jed put in. Bethany bit hard on her pipe.

'So now they work for someone else?' she said. 'So why don't you come to the point, gentlemen?' The way she inflected the word gentlemen suggested she was highly suspicious.

'We're trying to be helpful here, Mrs Bartok,' Jed said. 'We think we can bring your boy back to you safe and sound. How would that be?'

Bethany's lip trembled again.

'Why would you do that, Mr Cutaway?'

'Out of kindness, ma'am,' James Cutaway said. 'We don't like injustice. It's against our principles.'

Bethany looked at Sunshine; he raised an eyebrow.

'If you don't like injustice why did you send your boys to shoot out my windows?' she asked. James Cutaway grinned.

'Well, that wasn't our intention and we regret it. But those boys are kind of high-spirited and they sometimes get things a little out of proportion.'

'Well, maybe you'll tell them the next time they come I'm gonna shoot the hell out of them with my buffalo gun,' she said.

This time both the brothers grinned at her but they said nothing. Bethany took her pipe out of her mouth.

'So, what are you suggesting?' she asked directly.

Jed shook his head. 'What we want is to get your boy safely home to you.'

'And what do I do in return?' she asked.

'You sign over this farm to us legally for a fair price. That's all we ask.' James wasn't grinning any more.

'You mean you want for me to give up my home?' she asked in a high squeak of indignation.

'Not at all, Mrs Bartok,' Jed said. 'If we do this deal you can stay on this land for the rest of your days.'

Bethany's eyes popped with amazement.

'You mean you'd own it but I could live here?' she asked.

'That would be the deal,' Jed said, smiling now. 'We would write that into the agreement so it's all watertight and sealed.'

'You get your boy back and live here in peace and quiet, and we get to own the homestead,' James said.

There was a moment's silence. Bethany's jaw was chomping away as she considered the implications. Sunshine drained off the last of his beer.

'Why is this land so important to you, gentlemen?' he asked with a beguiling smile. Jed smiled back.

'That's a hard question, Mr Shining. Let's just say, we owned it way back and we sort of have an attachment to it.'

'It wouldn't be something to do with oil or gas, would it, Mr Cutaway?' Sunshine asked innocently.

Both Cutaways stared at him; they weren't smiling or grinning any more. James Cutaway turned to Bethany Bartok.

'D'you want your boy back, Mrs Bartok?' he asked.

'Yes, I do,' she said. For the first time Sunshine saw a weakening in her expression. Jed Cutaway nodded.

'Then think it over, Mrs Bartok,' he said. 'Think it over before it's too late.'

CHAPTER SIX

The two brothers thanked Bethany for the home brew and mounted up.

'Take good care to remember,' Jed Cutaway said. 'We'll come back tomorrow for your answer.' Then they rode back towards town.

Sunshine looked at Bethany and saw for the first time how deeply distressed she was. She placed her elbows on the table, lowered her head, and wept.

Sunshine looked down at her and his heart seemed to turn over in his chest.

'What am I gonna do?' she cried, 'and what's gonna happen to my poor boy?'

Sunshine laid a hand on her shoulder.

'That's a difficult question,' he said. 'But whatever the answer is, I'm here to help.' He sat down and considered their options.

'One thing's for sure,' he said. 'Those two Cutaway *hombres* know more about your badlands than we think. My guess is they see gold down there, enough to keep them as rich as Croesus for the rest of their lives. That means one thing: it can make you rich as well!'

She looked up at him through her tears.

'D'you think they can get my boy back for me?' she

asked. 'That's all I want.'

'That's what I'm trying to figure out, Mrs Bartok.' He looked away over the pasture. 'Tell me this: which is more valuable to you, your boy or the prospect of riches beyond your dreams?'

She thrust out her jaw and glared at him.

'How can you ask that?' she said. 'My boy's worth more to me than all the gold in California.'

'Well then,' he said, 'that's what we must work for. But if you play your cards right you might get them both.'

It was time to do the chores around the farmstead. Bethany gritted her teeth.

'If I don't look after the spread it ain't gonna look after itself, is it? And in any case, I think better while I'm working.'

She loaded her stubby pipe and lit up. 'Why don't I show you round and you can help as we go along? You might even have some bright ideas as we go.'

The first thing to do was to milk the cows. It was past time and they were all mooing impatiently.

'You ever milked a cow?' Bethany asked him.

'I don't believe I ever have,' he replied.

'Well, now's your chance to learn.'

They went out to the shed where the cows were all gathering, waiting to be milked, and Bethany gave him a lesson in milking.

'You get in on the right-hand side,' she instructed. 'You take the stool in your left hand, put your head against the cow's side, say a few kind words to her, put the bucket under the udder and then milk away, smooth but firm. Don't let the cow kick over the bucket or get a hoof in it. If she does that it spoils the milk and we don't want that nohow, do we?'

Sunshine watched as she gave a demonstration and he saw how gentle she was with the cows. She even used their names when she spoke to them and they responded as though they understood.

'These critters are not so dumb as you think,' she said. 'They understand a whole lot more than we think they do.'

'Just like my horse Chingalong,' he agreed, 'only he's even smarter.'

It was now time for Sunshine to try his hand, but before he could take his place there came the sound of voices and the jingle of harness. He went to the door and saw a gig stopping outside the door of the cabin. The driver got down and held out his hand to a lady. She was no more than twenty years old and she was dressed somewhat modestly but in fine-cut clothes.

'Great heavens above!' Bethany exclaimed from beside Sunshine. Then she rushed forward to embrace the lady. Sunshine put his pail aside and walked towards them.

'My, oh my!' Bethany said. She turned to Sunshine. 'This is my daughter Elspeth. She's come home.'

Sunshine, smiling, stood facing the young woman. He saw at once that she favoured her mother but was somewhat more handsome; he might have used the word *beautiful*, in fact.

'This is Mr Stubbs Shining,' Bethany introduced. 'He's helping on the farm.'

Elspeth stretched out her hand to Sunshine. Sunshine held it gently. It wasn't the hand of a working woman, but the soft hand of a scholar or a lady.

The driver of the gig unloaded a large case and carried it on his shoulder into the cabin.

'So you've come back to stay?' cried Bethany. Sunshine had never seen her so excited before.

'Well, this is home, isn't it?' Elspeth said. Sunshine noticed that her voice was mellow and low. The young woman went to the porch and sat down at the table.

'I can sure use a drink,' she said. 'It's been a long ride on the railway and the stage shook my bones up something terrible.'

Bethany rushed into the cabin and turned at the door.

'D'you think you can finish the milking?' she asked Sunshine.

'I can try,' Sunshine said. 'If I get it wrong you might be a little short on milk today.'

The young woman gave a musical laugh.

The driver of the gig was standing around as though waiting for something. Elspeth got her purse out and paid him.

'Why, thank you, missy,' he said. 'That's mighty generous of you.' He tucked the dollars away in his vest pocket and turned to Sunshine.

'I believe you're Mr Stubbs Shining,' he said. 'I heard how you upended that bully in the trough the other day and then shot him in the leg.'

'I was sorry I did that,' Sunshine confessed. 'The man was liquored up to his skull but I had to defend myself.'

'Sure you did. Only now I hear he's at death's door. I thought you should know that.'

'You mean he's likely to die?'

The gig driver scratched the back of his head.

'The sawbones is fighting to save him but they say it's just a matter of time. That wound has turned real bad.' The gig-man tipped his hat. 'I just thought you should know that, Mr Shining.'

Sunshine watched the gig drive away towards town, then went back into the cowshed to finish the milking. His head was in a whirl but he got on with the milking pretty well considering he was a novice. While he was working Bethany appeared at the door; she was laughing.

'It's so good to have Elspeth back,' she said. 'I think going East with those people was kind of disappointing, but now she's back and she wants to rest up, so I thought I'd come out and help with the chores. How you doing out here, anyway?'

'I'm learning fast,' he said.

She looked at him closely.

'You're looking a little yellow around the gills. Did the old gels kick you or something?'

He told her about the dying man.

'Well, that's real bad sass,' she said somewhat unsympathetically, 'but I guess that's the way it is out here in the wilderness. You have to defend yourself or you end up dead.'

'That may be true,' he said, 'but I want to ride into town and talk to him before he dies.'

Bethany looked a little bewildered.

'You mean you want to give Slam Smith the last rites or something?'

Sunshine creased his brow. 'I just have a hunch he might have something to say to me.'

Bethany nodded. 'Well, you're your own man, Sunshine, and so far your hunches have been pretty good for such a youngster. Why don't you ride into town after you've got something of substance in your belly and do what you have to do? But make good and sure you've packed that Peacemaker on your hip and got that Winchester of yourn loaded up good and ready just in case.'

They went back to the porch, sat down and drank milk fresh from the cows. Elspeth had changed her mind about resting

73

and she was looking out over the farmstead with relish.

'I could stay here for ever!' she said.

'Sit down, Ellie,' Bethany said. 'I have something to tell you.'

Elspeth sat down and listened while Bethany told her about her brother's kidnapping. Sunshine watched to see how Elspeth reacted and saw how her young brow knotted with concern.

'They won't kill him, will they?' she asked.

'They're asking for a thousand dollars, but that's only the beginning,' Bethany told her. Sunshine said nothing. After he had eaten, he decided to ride into town.

'Why don't I come with you?' Elspeth asked him. Bethany looked astonished.

'But you've only just got here,' she said. 'You need to rest up.'

Elspeth looked at Sunshine and nodded.

'I do feel a little tuckered out so maybe I should leave it till tomorrow.'

Sunshine looked at her and smiled. He saw what a high-spirited young woman she was, just like her ma. *How many women of any age would travel unaccompanied by rail?* he wondered. He saddled up Chingalong.

'We're riding into town again,' he said to the horse, 'but don't get yourself all tensed up, because it's going to be OK.'

'Take it easy,' Bethany shouted out, 'and make sure to keep that Colt revolver close by your side.'

Sunshine patted the holster and gave Bethany a wink.

'Don't worry, Mrs Bartok. Take good care of that daughter of yours.' He turned Chingalong's head and rode towards town.

Why am I doing this? he asked himself as he rode along. *Well, I guess I'm doing it to soothe my conscience some.*

He arrived in town just as the stores were pulling their shutters across. The first person he encountered was Sheriff McGiven, who was standing on Main Street with his thumbs in his suspenders.

'Why, good day, Mr Shining. What brings you into town?'

'Just doing a little visiting, Sheriff.'

'Anyone in particular?' the sheriff asked him.

'I thought I'd look in on Slam Smith, if he's around.'

Sheriff McGiven frowned. 'You might be lucky and you might not,' he said. 'Slam could be halfway to heaven or the other place by now.'

'Whichever way he's going, can you point me in the direction of the infirmary?'

The sheriff pointed his thumb over his shoulder.

'You'll find it down that way, a few paces towards the end of town.'

'Thank you, Sheriff.' The town was so small a few paces would take you right away into the creosote prairie land.

'By the way,' Sheriff McGiven said, 'after you've visited with what's left of Slam Smith, I'd like a word with you in my office.'

'I'll bear that in mind,' Sunshine said.

'You do that, Mr Shining,' the sheriff replied without the flicker of a smile.

Sunshine rode on to the end of town, where he saw a sign with the legend:

> Doctor Emmanuel Soskin,
> Bachelor of Medicine and own Infirmary

He dismounted and patted Chingalong on the head.

'Stay here, buddy. This is gonna be a tough assignment.' He walked across the sidewalk and rang the bell outside the door. Nobody seemed to be at home. He was about to ring again when the door was opened by a flustered-looking young woman dressed as a nurse.

'What do you want?' she demanded.

'Is Doctor Emmanuel Soskin available?' Sunshine asked.

'Who are you?' she asked abruptly.

'The name's Shining,' he said, 'Stubbs Shining. I'm enquiring about a certain Slam Smith.'

The nurse shook her head. 'You can't see Mr Smith,' she said. 'Right now the priest is with him and things don't look at all good.'

'I understand and I'm sorry,' Sunshine said. 'How about if I sit right here and wait while you see how the patient is?'

'Well, you can sit as long as you like, but I don't think it will do you much good, Mr Shining.'

'That's as maybe,' Sunshine said, 'but I think I'll wait all the same if you don't mind.'

The young woman closed the door and Sunshine sat on a bench under the ramada. He sat for a long time, then someone opened the door and came right out. It was a Catholic priest and he looked sort of thoughtful.

'Is it you who's waiting to see the dying man?' he asked Sunshine.

'Yes, sir, I am' Sunshine said. The priest looked wary.

'Well, I've just given him the last rites, so I think we should leave him in peace unless you're a close relation.'

Sunshine stood up. 'I'm just a well-wisher who shot him in the leg.'

'Well, there isn't much left of that leg now,' the priest

said. 'The doctor sawed it off early this morning.

'I'm sorry to hear that,' Sunshine said. The priest gave him a straight look.

'If you want me to hear your confession, why don't you come down to the mission?'

'Thanks for the offer,' Sunshine said, 'but I don't think I have time right now. So my soul must wait for a while longer.'

The priest nodded. 'God be with you, my son,' he said.

Sunshine watched him walk away and thought the word 'son' was somewhat inappropriate since the priest didn't look to be much more than forty years old himself.

Then the door opened again and the disagreeable young woman looked out.

'Ah, you're still here, Mr Shining. You can come in now.'

Sunshine walked into the dismal interior and came face to face with a man of around fifty.

'So you're Mr Stubbs Shining,' the man said. 'I'm Doctor Emmanuel Soskins.' He didn't hold out a hand. 'I hear you've come to enquire about the patient, Mr Slam Smith.'

'That's right, Doctor. How is Mr Smith?'

The doctor shook his head. 'I'm sorry to tell you he died less than five minutes ago.'

Sunshine looked at the doctor and saw no trace of emotion on his face.

'Well, I'm sorry about,' he said.

'I'd like to say he died peacefully,' the doctor replied, 'but I'm afraid the end was bitter and hard.'

'Well, at least the priest got here in time to hear his confession,' Sunshine said. The doctor gave him a thoughtful look.

'Just before he died, he said something strange.'

'Something strange?'

'I wouldn't mention it but he happened to say "Sunshine" and then something else that sounded like "stinking flats".'

'Stinking flats,' Sunshine repeated. 'You know why he said that?'

'I have no idea. People say all kinds of things when they're dying.'

'Well, thank you for telling me that, Doctor.'

Sunshine walked away from the infirmary and was about to mount Chingalong when someone called out his name. He turned to see the barber-cum-funeral director approaching.

'Good day, Mr Shining,' the barber said. 'I'm surprised to see you here.'

'I rode into town to enquire about Slam Smith, but I guess I was a little too late. He just died.'

The barber drew closer and grabbed him by the arm.

'You shouldn't have come here, Mr Shining. Slam's buddies are on the prowl and they're talking about revenge on the man who shot Slam. They're drinking in the saloon and getting themselves really wound up. You should get on that horse and ride out of town before they know you're here.'

'Well, thanks for the warning, sir.'

The barber nodded. 'Don't mention it, Mr Shining.' He turned to go into the infirmary.

'By the way,' Sunshine said. 'What do you know about "stinking flats"?'

The barber stopped abruptly and turned. 'Why do you want to know about Stinking Flats?'

Sunshine shook his head. 'Just a notion. Slam Smith mentioned it just before he died, so it must have been heavy on his mind.'

The barber looked to left and right, then came closer and said very quietly:

'I don't know much about Stinking Flats, except that it's a place not far from here.'

'Thank you,' Sunshine said. The barber stared at him for a moment.

'Who are you?' he asked in a low tone. 'Some kind of yellow-haired wizard?'

'Just a man passing through,' Sunshine said.

The barber shook his head and disappeared into the infirmary, presumably to measure up the dead man for his coffin.

Sunshine took Chingalong's reins and mounted up.

'Well, buddy, it's time we went back to the spread for some of Mrs Bethany Bartok's good cooking. And to renew our acquaintance with that real nice girl Elspeth Bartok, who is a deal prettier than her ma.'

He chuckled to himself as he rode in the direction of the saloon, but he didn't get far. As he came alongside the batwing doors they swung open and three men spilled out. They were laughing and slapping one another on the back and one of them was holding a revolver.

'I'm gonna plug that golden-haired boy right between the eyes,' he boasted.

The other two roared with laughter and staggered out on to Main Street.

'Not if I get there first,' one of them shouted, 'and I won't plug him between the eyes. I'll plug him lower down so he has to walk like this all the way to hell.' He did an imitation of a man trying to walk after he's been shot in the crotch.

Sunshine thought of turning Chingalong and heading out of town but it was too late. The third man, who appeared to be the most sober of the three, suddenly stopped and pointed in his direction.

'Why, lookee here,' he said. 'Ain't that the very boy hisself?'

Sunshine recognized him as Brad Bassington. The other two *hombres* suddenly stiffened and Sunshine saw that they were the same men as had gunned down on Bethany's spread the day he'd ridden in.

'What do I do now?' he muttered to himself.

'Get yourself down from that hoss and face the music,' the third gunman shouted. 'You shot our buddy Slam and now you have to pay the price.' He raised his gun and fired a shot in Sunshine's direction, but the shot went wide.

Sunshine weighed up the odds: one sober, inexperienced man against three highly experienced drunken gunmen. It would be like walking into the jaws of death. So what should he do?

The next second he knew the answer.

'Brace yourself for action,' he muttered between his teeth. He dug his heels into Chingalong's sides. Chingalong shuddered, then leaped forward and broke into a gallop. Two of the gunmen dodged to one side but the third, Brad Bassington, reached up and tried to grab Chingalong's reins. Sunshine had the Peacemaker in his hand and, as the man reached up he pistol-whipped him on the side of the head. The man fell like a stone under Chingalong's hoofs. Sunshine then fired a shot at another of the men; he fell back on the sidewalk. No time to think!

Sunshine leaned forward and rode hell for leather without looking back. The last thing he remembered seeing was Sheriff McGiven standing on Main Street, his mouth wide open in astonishment.

*

He galloped on down the trail towards the Bartok spread, then stopped and listened. There was no sound other than the soughing of the trees and the chirping of the birds.

'You did a mighty fine job there, Ching,' he said to the horse. 'If you hadn't acted quickly one of us would be dead by now.'

He found that he needed to catch his breath and suddenly realized his heart was beating fit to bust.

CHAPTER SEVEN

It was almost dark when he rode up to the cabin. Bethany came out on to the porch with her buffalo gun.

'Who's there?' she challenged.

'Not to worry, Mrs Bartok,' he shouted. 'It's only Sunshine, your blue-eyed boy.'

'Well, you'd better come right in,' she said. 'You've been gone so long I was beginning to be afraid you'd gone to the land of the departed.'

'You could have been right but luck was with me and I'm still here in the land of the living.' He dismounted and took Chingalong into the stable.

'You did well, my friend.' He patted the horse's neck. 'You've got a hell of a lot of horse sense, *mon ami*.' He returned to the cabin, where Elspeth rose to greet him. She looked more radiant than ever now she was rested up.

'Well then,' Bethany looked at him hard through her alert and eager eyes, 'did your hunches serve you well?'

'I'm still thinking on that,' he admitted, 'but I learned a lot.'

'Like what?' she asked.

'Like Slam Smith is dead. The wounded leg turned bad and the doc couldn't save him.' He told them about the priest giving Slam Smith the last rites and his encounter with the three gunmen.

'You mean they tried to kill you?' Elspeth cried, horrified.

'Well, they were a little too drunk to succeed in that,' Sunshine said, 'but it was a pretty close thing.' He told them how his quick thinking and Chingalong's speed had saved his life. Bethany reached for her pipe.

'This doesn't make a whole lot of sense, does it?'

'How'd you figure that?' Sunshine asked.

'Well, first Jed Cutaway offers you a job after you shot Slam Smith, and now Slam Smith's buddies are trying to kill you. How do you work that one out?'

Sunshine nodded and frowned.

'I've been trying to put that together all the way back from town and I don't know the answer. But one thing seems certain.'

Both women stared at him intently.

'What's that?' Bethany asked him.

'Nothing in the Cutaway camp is what it seems,' he said. 'When the Cutaway brothers came up to the house yesterday they said that their boys got a little out of hand at times. I think it's a lot more complicated than that.'

Bethany nodded: she was way ahead of him.

'What you're saying is the Cutaways have a rebellion on their hands.'

Sunshine nodded. 'I've been thinking about your son's kidnapping, Mrs Bartok.'

A look of pain flickered across Bethany's face.

'I think about it all the time,' she said. 'So tell me your thoughts, Mr Shining.'

'It seems to me that those Cutaways were surprised – or were pretending to be surprised – to learn about Bart's kidnapping, but I'm sure they know who the kidnappers are and why they kidnapped him. So when they offered to

83

find him, I believe they meant it. If you let them buy what you call the Badlands, they will bring Bart back to you.'

'So you think we should agree to their demands?' Elspeth wondered.

'Maybe you should talk to them,' Sunshine replied. 'But first I have a question. Have you ever heard of Stinking Flats?'

'Stinking Flats!' Bethany exclaimed. 'What's with Stinking Flats?'

'I'm not sure,' he said. 'It's just another of my crazy notions.' He told them how 'Stinking Flats' and 'Sunshine' had been Slam Smith's last words. 'He said them to the doc, but my guess is he meant them for the priest when he was making his confession.'

'What does that imply?' Elspeth asked.

'Well, a man doesn't lie when he's dying, does he? He's too busy thinking about the next world. So my guess is it was part of his confession and he got kind of muddled in the head.'

Both women stared at him intently.

'So the question is where or what is Stinking Flats?' he said.

Elspeth shook her head. 'I've heard of it but I don't know where it is.'

Bethany nodded. 'It's a place not far from here. Where is this leading us, Sunshine?'

'I don't know, but I guess it might be where the kid-nappers are holding your son Bart.'

For a few moments nobody said anything. Then Bethany asked:

'So what do we do?'

'The first thing we do,' Sunshine said, 'is locate Stinking Flats.'

'How can we do that?' Elspeth asked.

Sunshine shrugged. 'By riding into town again and making a few discreet enquiries.'

'How can you make discreet enquiries without meeting those gunmen again?' Elspeth wondered.

'That's a chance I have to take.'

Elspeth wrinkled her brow. 'I could ride in with you,' she said.

'You will do no such thing!' Bethany warned her. 'I'm already worried sick about your brother. If anything happened to you I'd die.'

'But Ma,' Elspeth said, 'you let me go East with those Venebles and I travelled back by train and then by gig. So how can you be so worried? If it helps to bring back Bart you should be pleased.'

Bethany reached out and touched Elspeth's arm.

'I'll think about it and at sunrise tomorrow I'll let you know the result.'

Sunshine looked at Elspeth and saw by her expression that it wouldn't make an ounce of difference either way because she'd already made up her mind. Elspeth didn't say much, but when she'd made up her mind there was no arguing with her. Maybe she was like her mother in that respect.

Next morning after a good hearty breakfast they hitched the horses to the buckboard, ready to drive into town. Bethany had relented because she was wise enough to see that Elspeth intended to drive in anyway.

'I've decided to give Chingalong a day of rest. He's seen enough rough dealings for a bit,' Sunshine said.

Elspeth laughed melodiously. 'You talk like that horse is human,' she said.

'That's because he is practically human,' Sunshine agreed. 'If it hadn't been for his quick thinking I might

85

have been as stiff as Slam Smith by now.'

Elspeth shook the reins and they set off down the trail to town.

'To tell you the truth, I'm real worried about my ma,' Elspeth said.

'I can see why. She's as tough as a trail boot but not as tough as she thinks she is.'

Elspeth gave that musical laugh again.

'It's a good thing you dropped by when you did. But I want to ask you something.'

'Well, please ask away. Bringing out the truth has a lot to recommend it.'

Elspeth hesitated. Then: 'I don't mean to be rude but, with all the danger and shooting and stuff, what's in this for you?'

'That's a good question and it deserves an honest answer.'

She turned to look at him and he felt a burning desire to kiss her on the lips.

'So what's the answer?'

'The answer is: I have no idea. I rode West because I wanted to open up my life. When I heard those gunmen shooting up your ma's cabin I had to stop. I guess it's what some people call Fate.'

'So do you think you're getting close to your goal?'

He felt her breath on his cheek

'I'm not sure,' he said quietly. 'That depends. . . .'

'On what?' she asked. *Was she teasing?* he wondered as they continued on their way.

They had been so deep in conversation that they hadn't seen the two men on horseback concealed among the birches a little to the right of the trail. After they had passed the two men, one of them large, the other smaller and both wearing heavy moustaches, emerged from the stand of birches and rode towards the Bartok homestead. When Sunshine and Elspeth drove into town many heads turned towards them in wonder. The pair pulled up outside the store and went inside.

'Why, good day, Miss Bartok,' Mr Snaze the toothy storekeeper said in surprise. 'How are we this morning?'

'I'm quite well, thank you, Mr Snaze,' Elspeth said. 'How is Mrs Snaze?'

'Well enough, well enough,' he said. 'Why don't you sit down and take a mug of that excellent coffee she brews up?'

'I believe I will, thank you.' Elspeth glanced at Sunshine, drew her skirts around her and sat down.

Until then they had been the only people in the store, but now a number of folk came trickling in; several of them stared at Sunshine with interest.

'Are you the boy who rode down on those men yester-day?' someone asked Sunshine.

'Well, I didn't exactly ride down on them,' he replied with a grin. 'They just stepped in the way of my horse.'

That gave rise to loud guffaws of laughter.

'Is that how one of them got a dent in the skull and another got a bullet in his shoulder?'

This was news to Sunshine but he was relieved to hear that no one had been killed.

'It was just a matter of self-defence,' he said. 'My horse Chingalong did most of the heavy work.'

'Except for the gunplay,' someone said and laughed. 'Your horse might be smart but he's not smart enough to handle a shooter, is he?'

'Where did you learn that?' another one asked him.

'It just came like a bird in the night,' Sunshine said.

'Some bird!'

There was more laughter.

Sunshine sat down at a table opposite Elspeth and Mrs Snaze served up hot steaming coffee; it was everything the storekeeper had promised.

'How's your ma?' Mrs Snaze asked.

'She's pretty hard-pushed at the moment considering everything,' Elspeth said.

'There must be a lot to do up at the spread since your dear pa passed away.'

'Sure is,' Elspeth agreed.

'Good job you came back and she's got Mr Shining here to help out.'

Sunshine smiled and said nothing.

'You heard anything from your brother Bart?' a man asked.

'Not lately,' Elspeth said, apparently without concern. She leaned forward to Mrs Snaze and spoke quietly. 'You happen to know where Stinking Flats is, Mrs Snaze?'

Mrs Snaze looked at her sharply, then sat down.

'Why do you want to know about Stinking Flats?' she asked apprehensively. 'It's not the sort of place a girl like you should be going. Like its name it smells bad, so they tell me.'

'Don't worry, Mrs Snaze, I've got my guardian angel to protect me.' Elspeth half-winked at Sunshine. Mrs Snaze considered for a moment.

'Why don't you come through to the back room and I'll draw you a map.'

The two women got up from the table and went through to the back room. The storekeeper came over and looked down at Sunshine.

'I heard you're working for the Cutaway brothers,' he said.

'Well, you don't want to believe every rumour you hear,

Mr Snaze. The truth is I've got enough to do helping out at the Bartok spread. A man can't have two masters, you know, or even mistresses for that matter.'

Snaze nodded and gave a toothy grin.

'That's true, Mr Shining, that's true. Where did you learn how to talk like that?'

'I did a fair amount of reading back East,' Sunshine said, 'and some of it stuck, I guess.'

Someone came into the store and stood close to the door.

'Good morning, Sheriff,' a voice said.

The sheriff looked around the store, then came over to Sunshine's table.

'So you're back, Mr Shining,' he said without smiling.

'Well, I'm sitting right here drinking a mug of excellent coffee, so I guess I must be,' Sunshine agreed with a grin. The sheriff shook his head solemnly.

'You think you're bullet-proof, Mr Shining?'

'No, I've just been lucky so far, Sheriff.'

'Well, I hope your luck holds out,' the sheriff replied. He breathed in slowly. 'I saw what happened yesterday, but I need to fill in on the details. So I wonder if you'd care to step over to my office before you leave town?'

Sunshine took a swig of Mrs Snaze's coffee.

'I'd be glad to, Sheriff, but why don't you just sit yourself down and have a mug of Mrs Snaze's strong coffee at my expense?'

A look of uncertainty clouded Sheriff McGiven's face, but only for a moment.

'Well, thank you,' he said, and sat down at the table.

The storekeeper was quick off the mark, especially when it came to business. So the steaming mug of coffee appeared almost immediately. McGiven sipped it cautiously, then nodded with satisfaction.

'Just as good as usual,' he said to Sunshine.

'My pleasure, Sheriff. Now why don't you tell me about those gun-toting drunks who tried to shoot me down yesterday?'

'Well, two of them are in the infirmary right now,' the sheriff said, 'and the third is probably sleeping like an angel – or a devil, depending on how you look at it. By the way, Slam Smith is to be put in the ground tomorrow morning at around eleven.'

'So, what can I tell you, Sheriff?'

'What I need,' said McGiven, 'is a signed statement from you about what happened. Then we can put the whole thing to bed.'

Though Sunshine didn't much care for the image of those gunmen lying in bed, he nodded.

'That seems a good idea, Sheriff.'

'I take it an educated man like you can write and sign his name?' the sheriff queried. Sunshine grinned.

'Tell me, Sheriff, how come Mr Jed Cutaway offered me a job after I shot Slam Smith in the leg? And another thing: how come those three gunmen tried to ventilate me if they're working for the Cutaway brothers?'

The sheriff looked somewhat puzzled.

'I can't discuss the Cutaway brothers, Mr Shining. That's way out of my territory.'

Sunshine was still smiling.

'What about the kidnapping of Brad Bartok? Is that way out of your territory too, Sheriff?'

At that moment Elspeth appeared, holding a sheet of paper.

'Why, good morning, Sheriff McGiven,' she said. McGiven rose from the table.

'Why, Miss Bartok, how good to see you. You're looking

quite stately.'

Elspeth gave him one of her most beguiling smiles. Sunshine could have sworn he saw the sheriff's face turn a slightly darker shade of purple.

'I'll just walk across to Sheriff McGiven's office,' Sunshine told her. 'I have to fill out a form.'

Elspeth nodded. 'I'll just talk to Mrs Snaze a little more,' she said.

Sunshine and the sheriff walked out under the overhang and stepped down on to Main Street. Sunshine paused for a moment to look left and right. There were quite a few folk riding or walking by, and one or two tipped their hats to the sheriff.

'I see you take care before crossing the street,' McGiven remarked.

'Well, I don't want to be run down by a horse, do I?' Sunshine replied. 'Could be a waste of life when I've got so much to do.'

The sheriff gave him a quizzical look.

They started walking across Main Street, which was very wide. When they were halfway across the sheriff suddenly stopped.

'Why, here come the two Cutaway brothers,' he said.

Looking to the right Sunshine saw the Cutaway brothers riding towards them. They were not alone: they had at least six other riders with them. The sheriff took off his wide-brimmed hat and gave a kind of shuffling bow, like he was greeting a king or the President of the United States.

'Why, good morning, Mr Cutaway,' he said with an obsequious grin.

'Good morning, McGiven,' Jed Cutaway replied.

James Cutaway said nothing, but his expression spoke

for him. He wasn't a generous or a welcoming man. Jed Cutaway switched his gaze to Sunshine.

'Ah, Mr Shining, so you're in town again.'

'Yes, I'm here on business,' Sunshine told him.

Jed Cutaway gave a quiet chuckle.

'I hear you put two men in the infirmary yesterday. You're getting quite a name for yourself, Mr Shining.'

'Well, Mr Cutaway, I guess those two drunks put themselves in the infirmary. I just helped them along a little.'

Jed Cutaway gave a sideways nod of appreciation.

'Why don't you just step into the saloon and take a drink with us? Me and my brother have things we'd like to discuss with you. Ain't that so, James?'

James gave a wry nod. 'That is so,' he agreed without enthusiasm.

Jed turned to the six riders escorting them.

'Take a drink, boys,' he said. 'It's gonna be a long hot day.'

Sunshine looked over the group but didn't recognize any of them. He saw that they were all tooled-up with shooters; they looked a pretty grim bunch.

'Why don't you come and take a drink as well, McGiven?' Jed Cutaway invited. 'Like I said, it's gonna be a hot day.'

'Why, thank you, Mr Cutaway.'

Sunshine looked at the sheriff and noticed he was blinking fast, which usually meant a man was nervous or about to tell a big lie. Sunshine then looked across Main Street and saw Elspeth standing outside the door of the store with Mrs Snaze. He raised his hand and cocked his head to one side. Elspeth raised her hand in acknowledgement.

'Who is that young woman?' Jed Cutaway asked.

'That's Miss Elspeth Bartok,' Sunshine told him.

'Why, so it is,' Jed Cutaway said. 'What a handsome creature she's become.'

The sheriff looked at Sunshine and blinked.

Then they all trooped into the saloon, where the saloon keeper swept off a table with a napkin.

'Please sit down, Mr Shining,' Jed Cutaway said. 'You too, McGiven.'

The two brothers, the sheriff and Sunshine sat down at the table. Sunshine noted that the six outriders walked right down through the saloon to the other end, where they made themselves comfortable, smoking cigarillos and drinking booze.

A waiter brought bottles of whiskey and glasses to the table and poured out the whiskey in generous measures. Jed Cutaway held up his glass.

'Here's to good business, gentlemen.'

'Here's to good business,' they replied.

Though Sunshine raised his glass he wondered what the 'business' was and why Elspeth wasn't sitting there with them.

'Well,' Jed Cutaway said, 'have you considered my offer, Mr Shining?'

Sunshine smiled. 'I've been thinking about it, sir. I've been thinking about it a lot.'

Jed Cutaway took a sip from his glass. 'And what are your conclusions, Mr Shining?'

Sunshine also took a sip of whiskey, then cleared his throat. It was good whiskey but a little too harsh for his taste buds.

'My conclusions are that I have an important job to do at the moment.'

'Indeed, sir. What would that be?' James Cutaway asked; there was a somewhat less friendly gleam in his eye.

Sunshine took another sip of whiskey and rolled it round in his mouth. Then he looked directly at James Cutaway.

'Right now,' he said, 'I'm fully occupied thinking about how I can find Bart Bartok and take him back to his mother.'

There was moment of silence. Sunshine was looking at each of the brothers in turn. They were staring right back without surprise or emotion. Then Jed Cutaway cleared his throat.

'I guess that's what we all want, Mr Shining.' He glanced at his brother, who gave a slight nod. Sunshine smiled one of his most radiant smiles.

'Well, gentlemen, I've discovered recently that I have a rare gift. I don't know where it came from or why it came but it gives me a lot of information.'

'About what?' James Cutaway asked, sceptically. He was obviously the more hard-nosed of the brothers and he didn't give a cuss about anyone.

'Well, for instance, I have a hunch about where they're holding Bart Bartok.'

Both brothers looked at Sunshine; for a moment neither of them spoke.

'So you know where they're holding Bart Bartok?' James asked him eventually. Sunshine tilted his head to one side.

'I don't know, Mr Cutaway. It's just a hunch, but I think you know where he's being held.' He looked directly into James Cutaway's eyes but James Cutaway didn't blink.

'Why do you say that, Mr Shining?' Jed Cutaway asked.

Sunshine nodded. 'What puzzles me is why you don't rescue that boy and take him back to his ma. At the moment she's suffering bad and she'd be awful grateful if you helped to get him back.' He turned to Sheriff

McGiven. 'My guess is you know too, Sheriff, so I'm wondering. . . .'

Sheriff McGiven started blinking as though he had grit in his eyes.

'Wondering what?' James Cutaway demanded bluntly.

'Wondering why you don't do something about it,' Sunshine said. 'I mean, if you know who's holding Bart and you don't do something to rescue him, it must be for some reason, mustn't it?'

'What reason would that be?' James Cutaway asked in a tone that held more than a hint of a threat.

Sunshine shrugged. 'That's what's puzzling me, Mr Cutaway. There could be a number of reasons.'

James Cutaway leaned forward across the table.

'Like what reasons?'

Sunshine met his gaze with a smile. 'Let me ask you something, Mr Cutaway.'

James Cutaway gave a slight nod but voiced no reply.

'OK, where's this leading to, Mr Shining?' his brother said. He was smiling but now it was more of a grin than a smile.

Sunshine sat back in his chair and considered matters. *Is this me asking all these questions?* he asked himself. He shook his head.

'Do you have any idea who those two moustachioed gents are who claim to be holding Bart Bartok? That's the first question.'

The two brothers were silent for a moment, but Sunshine saw them exchanging brief uneasy glances.

'What's the second question?' Jed Cutaway asked him.

'Well,' Sunshine said, 'this is more of a statement than a question. It seems to me those three *hombres* who gunned down on me yesterday and the unfortunate Slam Smith who died from a gunshot in the leg were all working for you. So why did they shoot Mrs Bartok's windows out and why don't you give a damn that Slam's dead and two of the others are in the infirmary.'

There was a tense silence.

'Like I said, the boys got a little out of hand,' Jed Cutaway said after a moment or two.

Sunshine nodded. 'Out of hand is one thing, Mr Cutaway, rebellion is something altogether different, and it's more than a matter of language, isn't it?'

Sunshine knew he was driving down a one-way street but he didn't rein in his horses.

James Cutaway leaned forward again and this time he glared at Sunshine.

'You're a smart young man, Mr Shining, but I think you're a little too smart for your cowboy boots.' He turned to Sheriff McGiven who was still blinking.

'Speaking of Slam Smith,' the sheriff said, 'there's a lot of things we need to get straight.' He took a deep breath. 'So I'm gonna ask you to hand in your artillery and walk right down to my office.'

Sunshine looked into the sheriff's eyes and saw him blink.

'Are you telling me I'm under arrest, Mr McGiven?'

The sheriff remained silent.

'I think that's what the sheriff said,' James Cutaway growled.

'On what charge?' Sunshine said, looking right back at James Cutaway.

McGiven was blinking quite fast now. 'Could be homicide,' he managed to bring out between tense lips. Sunshine smiled, but he didn't feel happy.

'Well now, Sheriff, I had the impression it was self-defence. When you shoot a man in the leg because he's trying to shoot you dead they usually call it self-defence. If

Slam Smith hadn't been so well pickled with alcohol at the time he might have been quick enough to shoot me first. Now, I wouldn't have cared too much for that, would I?' He looked first at the sheriff and then at the Cutaway brothers for a reply. James Cutaway and Sheriff McGiven looked baffled, but Jed Cutaway was faintly amused.

'You've sure got lip on you,' Jed Cutaway said. 'Did you ever think about going into the law business?'

Sunshine smiled at him. 'I have thought about it, Mr Cutaway,' he replied, 'but right now it isn't going to help much since Bart Bartok is still being held by some rather ornery *hombre* who don't give a shit about anything, especially when it comes to other men's lives.'

McGiven looked as though he was about to puke up his breakfast and James Cutaway looked angry but baffled. Nobody seemed to know what to say. Something had to give.

At that moment something did give, in the shape of a very attractive young woman who approached their table. It was Miss Elspeth Bartok.

CHAPTER EIGHT

Elspeth was a pretty smart young woman. She was not only smart but beautiful. At least that's what Sunshine thought, particularly at that moment. She had arrived just in the nick of time and she knew it. The men round the table all stood up like puppets pulled by invisible strings and looked at her intently but respectfully, which was unusual since unaccompanied ladies in bar rooms were often mistaken for calico queens.

Jed Cutaway gave her a particularly welcoming smile.

'Why, good day, Miss Elspeth,' he crowed. The sheriff didn't blink, he just went a deep vermilion colour. James Cutaway gave her a somewhat twisted grin of appreciation.

Elspeth curtsied graciously and looked at Sunshine.

'Why, Mr Shining, I've been waiting over there for so long I thought you were set to spend the night here in the saloon.'

Sunshine was standing with his hat in his hand.

'Well, Miss Elspeth,' he drawled, 'I'm right sorry to have kept you waiting. The truth is, I've been discussing business with these gentlemen.'

Elspeth raised an eyebrow.

'Indeed, what business would that be?' she asked sweetly.

Sunshine gave a slight bow and said, 'We've been thinking about your brother Bart and how we can rescue him.'

'Indeed,' she repeated in a strangely artificial tone.

Sunshine looked at her and wondered where she had learned to act so well. It was as though they were in a play. Romeo and Juliet sprang to mind.

'Why don't you sit down and join us in some refreshment, Miss Elspeth?' Sunshine heard Sheriff McGiven say in a somewhat stagey tone. Maybe he saw her intervention as his own rescue from a somewhat tricky situation.

A waiter rushed forward, bowed and brought up a spare chair, which he dusted down with a napkin. The outriders sitting at the other end of the saloon opened their mouths in astonishment and one of them let out a low whistle.

The waiter held the chair ready while Elspeth arranged her long skirt and sat down. Then she ordered a sarsaparilla and nobody turned a hair.

'Well now, gentlemen, this has gone on long enough, so what are you going to do about it?' she asked.

'What are we gonna do about what?' James Cutaway growled suspiciously.

She turned her large lustrous eyes on him.

'What are you going to do about rescuing my brother from those vicious men who are holding him captive?'

Vicious men who are holding him captive Sunshine thought to himself: *Where did she learn to talk like that?*

The two brothers exchanged glances. Then Jed spoke up,

'As soon as we know who's holding him and where they're holding him we'll make sure he's freed,' he assured her.

'Well, gentlemen, I think I can help you there,' Elspeth said.

99

'You mean you know where he's being held?' Jed Cutaway asked.

Elspeth sipped her sarsaparilla and smiled. Sunshine was amazed by her poise, considering the situation in which she found herself.

'Did you ever hear of Stinking Flats, gentlemen?' she asked.

It was as though someone had broken wind in public. The Cutaways looked at her in amazement and Sheriff McGiven gave a start.

'You mean . . . Stinking Flats?' he said.

'I think that's what I said,' Elspeth replied.

'Stinking Flats is an awesome place,' Jed Cutaway said. 'It's a real stinking swamp, like it says, and a man could sink right down and disappear before he could cry out for help.' He turned to his brother. 'You remember old Jed Butcher?'

James Cutaway gave a macabre grin. 'I remember Butcher well.'

'What happened to Mr Butcher?' Sunshine asked.

'Well, nobody knows for sure,' Jed said. 'Old Jed built a small cabin there. He didn't give a damn about the rumours or what the Injuns said about the place. He'd go and live there on his own. He used to ride into town on his mule every so often for supplies but one day he stopped . . . and nobody has ever seen him or his mule since.'

There was a pause.

'You know where his cabin is?' Elspeth asked.

Sunshine saw expressions of horror and suspicion flit across the faces of the Cutaway brothers and the sheriff's jaws were working like he had something distasteful in his mouth.

'You can't go there, Miss Elspeth,' McGiven said.

'Why not?' she asked. Now the sheriff was trying to

swallow the piece of gristle in his mouth.

'Because it ain't safe for man or woman. Certainly woman.'

'Are you challenging me to go there?' she asked him. The sheriff blushed purple.

'I'm just saying it wouldn't be advisable,' he said.

James Cutaway stirred himself. 'I don't believe they're holding your brother in Stinking Flats, Miss Bartok. I have a notion it's somewhere else entirely.'

'Then maybe you know where he *is* being held?' Elspeth said. James Cutaway slanted his head to one side.

'I think that's just a ruse to throw you off the scent.'

'OK,' she said. 'Then why don't you tell me *where* they are holding him?'

The brothers exchanged glances again.

Jed said, 'We'd like to be helpful on that and I'll guarantee one thing. If you use your influence with your ma to sell us that piece of land she calls the Badlands we'll deliver your brother safe and sound before you can turn round and say good morning, Mister Sun.'

Now Elspeth was looking at Sunshine.

'Well,' Sunshine said, 'I think we have to talk to Mrs Bartok about that.'

Jed smiled. 'Why don't you do that, Mr Shining?' he said.

Since nothing more was said about placing Sunshine under arrest, he and Elspeth walked out of the saloon and across Main Street to where the buckboard horses were drinking at the trough.

'So,' Sunshine said, 'you saved me from being locked up in the town jail. Thank you; that was a good move. I can't stand jail food, anyway.'

101

'You think the sheriff really would have locked you up?' Elspeth asked.

'I think that dumb sheriff does everything and anything the brothers tell him to do.'

'So what do we do now?' she asked.

Sunshine shrugged. 'I guess we ride back to the farmstead and talk to your ma.'

'So you think she should agree to their terms?'

'The main thing is we get your brother back in one piece. If that means selling off the land, maybe your ma should consider it, depending what price they offer.'

They started down the trail towards the Bartok spread.

'Where did you learn to deal with men like that?' he asked her as they rode along.

'Where did you learn to talk like that?' she countered.

They looked at one another and smiled. Sunshine felt his heart turn over.

'I learned a lot back East,' she said. 'They wanted me to stay and train as a teacher, but I didn't think that was quite my style. I'd like to be a lawyer, but that wouldn't be quite seemly for a woman, would it?'

Sunshine nodded. 'My kin wanted me to become a lawyer, and maybe I will if I go back East.'

'Are you planning on going back East?'

'It depends.'

'On what?' she asked.

He turned to look at her but she didn't lower her head or blush; she just looked right back at him.

'You know what,' he said. 'We'd make a real good team, you with your fine brain and me with my way of talking.'

Then she did blush and he felt an overwhelming desire to kiss her. But as he leaned closer they heard the sound of horses approaching.

'That's Mr Gibson,' Elspeth said. 'He's our neighbour.'

Sunshine watched as the man approached. He was rangy and bony and looked as tough as old rawhide – a typical Western farming man.

'Why, good afternoon, Miss Elspeth,' Mr Gibson said, raising his battered hat. 'So you're back among us. My word, you do look smart!'

'Thank you, Mr Gibson. How are you doing today?'

'I'm doing real well,' he said. 'How is your ma? I haven't seen her around lately.'

'Oh, she's bearing up well, Mr Gibson. How is Mrs Gibson?'

He gave her a hillbilly smile. 'Oh, she's well, apart from the bunions and the rheumatics, you know.' He looked at Sunshine. 'Howdy, you must be the boy who's helping out around the farm'. He reached across and offered his hand, which was big and bony like the rest of him. 'I see you're carrying a gun, boy.'

'I don't normally carry a gun,' Sunshine said. 'But you just don't know who you will meet out here these days.'

'True, true,' said the man. 'Why don't you all come up to my place fer the shindig come Sunday next?'

'We might just do that, Mr Gibson,' Elspeth said. Gibson screwed up his face and nodded.

'Good, good.' He edged his horse a little closer and looked off to the left towards a stand of cottonwoods. 'Hope you don't mind me mentioning it, Miss Elspeth, but has your ma put the farm up for sale?'

'Why do you ask, Mr Gibson?'

'Well now . . . hucks,' he said with embarrassment. 'I don't want you thinking I'm sticking my nose where it's not wanted here, but there's rumours circling around like big black buzzards in the sky.'

'What do those big black buzzards say?' Elspeth asked him.

'Well . . .' the poor man flushed red with embarrassment. 'I don't like interfering or nothing, that ain't my style.'

Elspeth flashed him a smile. 'Everyone knows that, Mr Gibson. Please tell me about those rumours.'

He leaned forward a little more. 'Well, Miss Elspeth, rumour has it that your brother Bart has been kidnapped.' Then he seemed to shrink back like a snail into its shell. 'Mind you, I don't listen none to rumours, Miss Elspeth.'

'Of course not.' Elspeth was still smiling. 'And I can tell you something: my mother has no intention of selling the farm. But the rumours about my brother are right; he has been kidnapped.'

Mr Gibson put on a shocked expression, but he wasn't much of an actor and Sunshine wasn't convinced.

'Let me ask you something, Mr Gibson,' he said. 'Who started these rumours?'

Gibson gave a furtive grin. 'Well, sir, rumours are rumours. You don't know who starts them or where they come from. They just come circling through the air, you know.'

'Like those big black buzzards you just mentioned,' Elspeth said.

Gibson put an index finger against his nose and looked off into the trees again.

'It's just that I seed them,' he muttered.

'What did you see – those big birds?' Sunshine asked him.

Mr Gibson looked somewhat agitated. 'I seed two men.'

'You saw two men?' Sunshine repeated. 'When did you see them, Mr Gibson?'

Gibson gave another furtive grin. 'I seen them at least twice around here.'

'Why don't you tell us about it, Mr Gibson?' Elspeth asked. Gibson's grin turned even more furtive.

'I don't want you to think I go spying on folk, Miss Elspeth. That's the last thing I want.'

Elspeth shook her head. 'You don't need to worry about that, Mr Gibson. Tell me, what did those men look like?'

'Well . . .' he tilted his head to one side, 'fact is, there were two of them. One of them was awful big and the other was much smaller and they both had terrible wide bushy moustaches on their faces.'

Sunshine looked at Elspeth. 'When did you see them?' he asked.

Gibson brightened up as though a sunbeam had struck his face.

'Oh, I seed them just before I met you.'

'You mean you met them on the trail?'

'Well, not exactly. I just seed them, but when they saw me they just skedaddled off the trail and into the trees. Tell you the truth, I don't think they knew I'd seed them.' He moved uneasily in the saddle. ' 'Course, I knew who they were 'cause I'd seen them before.'

'You'd seen them before?' Elspeth queried. Gibson gave a knowing nod.

'Well, you know, Miss Elspeth, I like to keep a watch on the birds and the beasts. I've been like it since I was half knee-high to a grasshopper. So I always carry my spyglass around with me and that's how I seed them.'

'So have you seen them often?' Elspeth asked him.

Gibson nodded. 'Why sure, Miss Elspeth, I seen them around here a few times. And another thing, Miss Elspeth. Those men always carry shooters with them as though they want to put the frights on folk. So I put two and two together and wonder what they're doing around here, you know.'

Elspeth smiled. 'Well, thank you, Mr Gibson,' she said.

Gibson grinned. 'It's been a real pleasure meeting you again, Miss Elspeth. You take care now.'

He crammed his battered hat on his head and rode on.

'What do you make of that?' Elspeth asked Sunshine.

Sunshine wasn't smiling.

'I think we have to get back to the farm as quickly as may be,' he said.

Elspeth whipped up the team and the buckboard moved on. They hadn't gone far before something unexpected happened. A shot rang out and a bullet whined so close to Sunshine that it almost took off his hat.

What's happening? he asked himself.

But Elspeth was way ahead of him and she pulled the team to a sudden halt.

'Get down,' she said. She flung herself over the side of the buckboard and pointed her Winchester over the top to where the shot had come from.

Sunshine leapt from the buckboard and was crouching on the other side as a second shot came whining in. He drew the Peacemaker and held it steady, watching for another flash, but none came.

'That was close,' he said.

'You're exposed there,' he heard Elspeth say. 'Why don't you come round here?'

Sunshine didn't need a second invitation. He scrambled round to the other side of the buckboard and joined her. Together they peered over the edge of the buckboard towards the trees on the other side.

'So what was that about?' Elspeth wondered, and once again Sunshine was amazed; she seemed so cool.

106

'That was about bad shooting,' he said. 'An inch or two lower and you'd have been scooping up my brains.'

'So you think they just wanted to scare us?' she asked. Sunshine shook his head.

'They certainly meant to do that,' he agreed. 'I guess we'd better get back pronto, see what's happened to your ma. But hold on a minute. I'm going over there to see if those varmints are still around.'

'I'm not sure that's a good idea,' Elspeth said.

'Why don't you cover me with that Winchester?' he suggested. 'But don't shoot me in the back because I've still got a few more things to do before I shuffle off this mortal coil.'

Elspeth stretched out on the buckboard with the Winchester pointing at the trees.

But before Sunshine could move across to the treeline he stopped suddenly and swung to the right.

'There's someone on the trail,' he said.

Yes, there was someone and he was riding quickly in their direction. Sunshine thought it might be one of the moustachioed gents, but to his surprise, he recognized Mr Gibson. Gibson rode right up to the buckboard and peered into the woods.

'Was that you fired those shots?' he shouted.

'Someone fired at us from the trees over yonder,' Elspeth told him.

'Well, I'll be damned!' Gibson said. 'That must have been those two *hombres* with bushy moustaches I seed earlier. Why would they do that?'

'Well, they have their reasons,' Sunshine said. 'And whatever they are, they're not too helpful for us.'

'I guess they might be still around,' Gibson said. 'Let's take a looksee.' He jigged his horse over to the margin of the trees where the shots had come from and dismounted.

Sunshine followed on foot with the Peacemaker pointing towards where the shots had come from. Gibson was peering about among the trees.

'Yep, that's them,' he said. 'Lookee here, this is where they were when they fired at you.'

Sunshine studied the ground but noticed nothing unusual.

'You figure this is it?' he asked.

'This is it,' Gibson insisted. 'This is where the horses stood and this here is where the two *hombres* crouched down and took a shot at you.'

When Sunshine looked more closely he could see what he had been blind to before: the imprint of the horses' hoofs and the slight impression on the ground where the men had crouched.

'Yes, that's them,' Gibson said. 'Lookee here. This is where the big *hombre* crouched and this here is where the small *hombre* crouched.'

'So there were definitely two,' Sunshine said.

'You can bet your life on that,' Gibson said, 'and it was those two gun-toting *hombres* I seed earlier.' He turned to look at Sunshine. 'Why would they want to shoot at you like that?'

'That,' Sunshine said, 'is the question. D'you think you could follow their tracks.'

Gibson gave that sly smile of his. 'Oh, I could track them, Mr Shining, I sure could, but right now I'm more worried about Mrs Bartok and what might have happened to her.'

Then Elspeth spoke. 'I think we should get back to the farm as soon as possible,' she said with some urgency.

'That's right, Miss Elspeth,' Gibson said, 'and I'm riding right back with you to make sure everything's hunky-dory.'

Sunshine and Elspeth climbed aboard the buckboard and headed back to the farm with Gibson riding slightly ahead. Sunshine wasn't taking any chances. He sat with the Peacemaker cradled on his lap, looking to left and right.

When they reached the spread Bethany Bartok was nowhere to be seen.

'D'you think your ma's OK?' Gibson asked anxiously.

Sunshine got down from the buckboard with the gun in his hand, and at that moment Bethany Bartok appeared with her buffalo gun.

'Well, thank the Lord!' she said. 'I thought those two varmints had come back to put the frighteners on me.'

'Have they been here?' Elspeth asked her.

'Just left no more than half an hour back.' She nodded at Gibson. 'Why, Mr Gibson, how good to see you,' she declared.

Gibson gave his hillbilly grin. 'Just came to see you're all right,' he said.

'Well, I'm right relieved to see you,' she said. 'Why don't you come right into the cabin and take a little refreshment?'

They went into the cabin and sat down while Bethany served her home brew. Sunshine saw that her hand was shaking.

'So those two gents appeared again?' he said. 'Did they say anything?'

Bethany took a quick look at Gibson and gave a curt nod.

'What they said, I don't quite know how to repeat.'

Elspeth took a deep breath. 'You mean about Bart?'

Bethany nodded again. 'They said if I didn't sign over the farm to them Bart might be put to death.' Then she bit

109

her lip and tried not to cry, but it was too late. She sat down at the table, put her head in her hands and shook with grief. Elspeth immediately sat beside her and put her arms around her. Though she didn't actually burst into tears herself, Sunshine could see how difficult she was finding it to hold them back.

He looked at Gibson and saw a whole lot of emotions struggling to get control of his face.

'W-well now,' Gibson stammered. 'Well now, Mrs Bartok, we surely have to get Bart back just as soon as we can.'

Nobody said anything more for a little while. Then when they had all got control of their emotions Elspeth ventured to ask:

'So what happened after that?'

'Well, I had to agree, didn't I?' said Bethany. She was looking at least ten years older now. 'As long as Bart is freed it doesn't matter what happens to me. I'll just fade right out of the picture.'

She said this without a trace of self-pity.

Gibson shook his head.

'Did you sign anything, Mrs Bartok?'

'Well, yes, I signed a letter that they put in front of me. I had to.'

Gibson suddenly transformed himself from a hick hill-billy into a man of action.

'Now, Mrs Bartok, we have to do something about this, not next week but right *now*.' His voice couldn't have been stronger or more determined.

Sunshine was impressed but also a little apprehensive. What happens when a rawboned farmer like Gibson gets it into his head to take action? *A bull in a china shop* came to mind.

'What would be your plan?' he asked Gibson. A look of

grim determination swept across Gibson's face.

'We have to find out where those galoots are holding Bart, don't we?'

'Have you ever heard of Stinking Flats?' Sunshine asked him.

'Stinking Flats?' Gibson echoed. 'What's with Stinking Flats?'

Elspeth intervened. 'We have a suspicion that that's where they're holding Bart.'

Gibson turned the thought over in his mind as though examining it from all angles.

'Stinking Flats,' he said again. 'That's where a man called Butcher lived.'

'So you've heard of him?' Sunshine said. Gibson wrinkled his brow.

'Oh, I knew Butcher. A real weird guy, half out of this world. Disappeared one day with his mule. Nobody knows where he went or why he disappeared.' He looked at Sunshine. 'Why d'you think Bart might be held there?'

Sunshine shook his head. 'It's just a hunch.' He told Gibson about Slam Smith's confession and how the Cutaway brothers had reacted to the suggestion.

Gibson half-closed his eyes. 'What do you think about this, Mrs Bartok? Did those scumbags say they were coming right back?'

Bethany nodded. 'They said they'd bring Bart right back to the farm and bring a man of the law, so I could sign the deed and make over the property.'

'Well now, Mrs Bartok,' Gibson said, 'I don't think it will happen that way.'

Bethany gave him a shrewd look. 'I'm beginning to think you're right,' she said.

'And it's starting to make sense to me too,' Elspeth said. 'Those two gents aren't going to expose themselves.

They're a whole lot too cunning for that.'

Sunshine agreed. 'That's why they bushwhacked us on the trail today.'

Elspeth told Bethany what had happened earlier.

'Which means they meant to kill us,' Sunshine said. 'So it's a good job they're such bad shots.'

'This land of yours must be mighty valuable,' Gibson said. 'I wonder why that would be?'

CHAPTER NINE

'Whatever you decide to do,' Gibson said, 'I have to tell you, Mrs Bartok, that I'm right with you.'

'Well, you can read the signs, Mr Gibson,' Sunshine said, 'so maybe you could lead us to Stinking Flats.'

Gibson wasn't a handsome man and he didn't shave very frequently, but now he looked extremely thoughtful.

'I could lead you there, Mr Shining, but I'm not sure if that's the best idea.'

'Then what d'you think we should do?' Elspeth asked him. Gibson looked concerned.

'Well, I have a suggestion to make. Those skookums won't kill your son, Mrs Bartok. That's 'cause he's a bargaining chip. Whoever's holding him wants your land real bad.'

Sunshine looked at Gibson with growing respect. The man was far from being the fool he had earlier seemed to be.

'So what do you suggest?' he asked. Gibson screwed up his face in concentration.

'What we do is wait. My guess is they'll come back soon enough. This is tough for you, I know, but it can't be helped.'

'But suppose they do kill my boy?' Bethany said in alarm.

'Like I said, as long as he's a bargaining chip they won't want to kill him. They'll just keep him some place safe and we don't know where that is. So what I think is: you all sit tight and wait while I watch and keep a lookout from that bluff up there with my spyglass. When I see them I can keep a track on them and then we'll find out where they're holding your son Bart.'

There was a pause and it was indeed pregnant. Bethany moved her fingers restlessly across the table and Sunshine and Elspeth exchanged worried looks.

'You mean we just sit here and wait?' Elspeth asked.

Gibson shrugged. 'I think that's the best plan, Miss Elspeth. If we start beating up on those guys it might be bad for Bart, but if we play along with them, they'll think they've won out on us.'

'What about you?' Elspeth asked. 'You can't just sit up there on the bluff and wait for things to happen. You've got your own farm to run.'

To everyone's surprise Gibson opened his mouth and let out a huge guffaw.

'You don't need to worry none about that, Miss Elspeth. I've got so many folk on the spread I don't need to do a danged thing. So I'm sort of put out to grass. That's how I get to watch the birds and the beasts. I might just as well be watching human folk as well, specially if it helps to free your boy Bart.'

Bethany looked thoughtful and then relieved.

'Well, thank you, Mr Gibson. That's real neighbourly of you. I think we have to agree on that.'

Gibson gave a slanting grin. 'Why don't you call me Jeremiah?' he said.

'Thank you, Jeremiah,' Bethany said with a smile.

Sunshine felt none too easy at the thought of doing nothing, But there was plenty to do around the farm so he and Elspeth just got stuck into it. Elspeth volunteered to help with the cooking and she proved to be more than adequate. Sunshine spent most of his time out on the farm, looking after the stock and tending the horses. Every day he rode Chingalong round the perimeter of the farm, which was more extensive than he had expected.

'Well now, Chingalong boy, d'you think we have a hope of winning this one?'

Chingalong tossed his head.

'I'm inclined to agree with you, hoss,' Sunshine said. He looked up at the bluff where he guessed Jeremiah Gibson was perched and watching him through his spy-glass.

Two days passed and all three of them were getting restless and irritable. Elspeth and her mother were almost at one another's throats. Then on the third morning as they were sitting at breakfast they heard the sound of horses approaching and the two moustachioed *hombres* appeared at the door.

Keep yourself still, Sunshine thought to himself, *and look meek.*

Elspeth opened the door.

'Good morning, gentlemen,' she said. Her voice sounded almost friendly.

Bethany was busy at the stove. When she turned Sunshine saw that she was trembling, either with fear or with anger, or possibly both.

'Why don't you sit down, gentlemen?' Elspeth said.

'I think we'll just stand if you don't mind,' the smaller of the men said without the flicker of a smile. The heavier man grinned and nodded.

'Have you thought about your promise, Mrs Bartok?'

Bethany stared at him defiantly. 'I've been thinking

115

about it all the time. Where's my son?'

The smaller man spoke again. 'Your son is quite safe, Mrs Bartok.'

'So far,' added the heavier man grimly.

Sunshine stiffened but said nothing. He thought of the Colt revolver near at hand and his fingers twitched in anticipation. Bethany was still staring at the two men.

'When will you bring my son back to me safely?' she demanded.

'Well, Mrs Bartok,' the lighter *hombre* said, 'we have a small difficulty here.'

'What sort of difficulty?' she asked. The lighter man held up a paper.

'You see, Mrs Bartok, this paper you signed might not be properly legal.'

'So, what are you going to do about that?' Elspeth asked him.

The two men exchanged glances.

'What we're gonna do,' the lighter man said, 'is we're gonna bring our lawyer with a properly authorized document for you to sign and then you can have your son back.'

'When will that be?' Bethany asked him. The big man was looking at Sunshine.

'We can't say exactly when,' he said, 'but it will be real soon.'

The two men edged towards the door.

'Think about it, Mrs Bartok, think about it,' the lighter man said.

They watched the two men ride away.

'I'd like to track down on those guys.' Sunshine said.

'That's just what they'll expect,' Elspeth warned, 'and they won't think twice about shooting you down.'

'I wonder if Jeremiah Gibson is watching up there?' Bethany speculated. Sunshine saw that she was close to tears again.

'Well, we won't know that for a while,' Elspeth said, 'but my guess is he will be.'

It had been a strange feeling, talking to those men who only a day or two earlier had tried to kill them.

They waited so long it was almost sunset. Then Jeremiah Gibson rode up to the cabin and dismounted. He was wearing leather chaps and he had a Winchester across his saddle; he looked ready for whatever the world might throw at him. He walked right into the cabin and nodded grimly.

'Well now, Mrs Bartok, I seen those *hombres* like I said. I think I know where they're headed and it ain't Stinking Flats.'

'You mean you know where they're holding Bart?' Bethany said. He gave a secretive grin.

'I believe I do, Mrs Bartok, I believe I do.'

It was time to discuss tactics. The question was, who would follow the trail and who would stay to look after the farm?

'I want to go,' Bethany declared. 'This has gone on long enough and I want to rescue my boy.'

'Well, that's as maybe,' Jeremiah Gibson declared, 'but we have to use our wits here, Mrs Bartok.'

'Well, I can bring my buffalo gun,' she said aggressively, 'and smoke them out.'

'Now steady on, Mrs Bartok!' Gibson cautioned. 'We can't just go blasting our way in there if we want to bring back your boy alive. What we have to do is use our brain matter. And anyways, you've got the farm to look after.' He looked at Elspeth. 'You too, Miss Elspeth. The best thing you can do is stay here and help your ma.'

Then he switched to Sunshine. 'And you, Mr Shining. I'm sure you'd like to be in on this. But don't worry none 'cause I have a few favours I can call on. So it won't be just us; it will be one or two of the boys. They'll be right glad to help out.'

He looked around to see how the others were responding. 'So I suggest you leave me to round them up and we'll hit the trail just after sunup tomorrow morning.'

So it was agreed, though Elspeth and Bethany looked really down-mouthed, since they had wanted to be on the trail with the menfolk.

Soon after sunup next morning Jeremiah Gibson appeared with three of his buddies: Jordan Rivers, Slim Savage and Jon Jenson. All were homesteaders and all were tooled up with various weapons: shotguns, old-time cap-and-ball pistols, and one prewar pistol of uncertain vintage.

'These boys are here to help, Mrs Bartok,' Jeremiah Gibson explained. Elspeth looked at Sunshine and shook her head.

'Take care of yourself,' she said and gave him a quick kiss on the cheek. The so-called 'boys' all raised their eyebrows knowingly.

'Now, boys,' Jeremiah Gibson said when Sunshine had appeared, ready and mounted up on Chingalong, 'you know the rules. Nobody shoots off their guns unless I say so – and I hope we don't have to – but these skookums don't give a damn for anyone, so be ready for whatever might happen.'

'Are the Cutaways involved in this?' Jordan Rivers piped up.

Jeremiah Gibson didn't know what to say. He looked at Sunshine.

'We don't know the answer to that, Mr Rivers. The only thing we're interested in is freeing Brad Bartok and bringing him home safe.'

'That's right,' Jeremiah Gibson agreed. 'So what we do is ride along without making too much jingle-jangle, 'cause we don't want to attract unnecessary attention. I'll lead the way.'

They set off down the trail with Gibson in the lead. Sunshine was content to bring up the rear on Chingalong, who seemed happy to tail the other horses. After quite a short ride along the marked trail Gibson held up one arm and they all came to a halt.

'Now, boys,' he said quietly, 'this is where we branch off the trail.' He pointed away into the aspens. 'This is where those skookums took off from the trail yesterday and I followed them.'

'You know where they were headed, Jeremiah?' Jordan Rivers asked.

'I have a strong feeling about that, Jordan,' Gibson replied.

'Couldn't be the Stanley Sheffield place, could it?' Rivers wondered.

Gibson tilted his head to one side. 'It could be, but then again it might not,' he said.

'Well, no one lives there any more,' Jordan said, 'not since Sheffield went bust and blew out his own brains. My guess is the Cutaway boys are using it to store cattle feed.'

Sunshine had keen ears and had been listening intently. Suddenly he said:

'Listen, I can hear riders coming!'

Jeremiah Gibson leaned down to get his ear closer to the ground.

119

'You're damn right, boy. Get your horses into that stand of trees and keep them dead quiet.'

The men lost no time in getting themselves off the trail and into the trees, where they waited like statues to see who was passing on the trail.

Seven riders came jogging along. They were obviously in no particular hurry.

'Well, my boots and buttons!' exclaimed Jordan Rivers after they'd passed. 'Did you see who that was?'

'We saw good and clear,' Jeremiah Gibson said. 'That was James Cutaway and his sidekicks.' He looked at Sunshine. 'What I'd like to know is: where are they headed?'

'They could be headed for the Bartok spread,' Sunshine speculated.

'So, what do we do now?' Jordan asked.

For the first time Jeremiah Gibson looked confused. The men turned to Sunshine and he considered their options. Either they could follow the James Cutaway bunch or they could continue on to the Sheffield place to establish the truth about Bart Bartok.

'I think we should go on,' Sunshine said. 'The Cutaways aren't going to harm those ladies and if we can find out where Bart is we have an ace in the hole.'

Jeremiah nodded solemnly. 'I think you're right on that, son,' he said.

They continued on for a mile or so. Then Jeremiah held up his hand and again they drew to a halt.

'Now, boys,' he said. 'The Sheffield place is some piece ahead. So I suggest you boys take a rest here while I go on and take a looksee. Then I'll come back and, depending on what I've found, we can decide on our next move.'

'Either that,' Jordan said, 'or we can leave our hosses

here and go forward on foot.'

'I think that might be the best idea,' Sunshine said.

So they tethered their mounts in a shaded glade where they could crop the grass and rest. Then they fanned out and made their way cautiously towards the Sheffield place, keeping off the faint track. From time to time Jeremiah Gibson went back to the track and bent down to examine the signs.

'This is the way, sure enough,' he said quietly. 'Lookee here. These are the hoofmarks. Two men on horses. This is the way they came.'

'Yep,' Jordan said, 'this is definitely the way to the Sheffield place.'

They got off the track again and made their way through the trees cautiously until Jeremiah waved them down again.

'Now, boys,' he said, 'get down on your bellies and edge forward through the trees. Keep as quiet as the dead.'

The 'boys' got down and slid forward from cover to cover. Then Jeremiah waved them to a halt again. He produced his spyglass and stood behind a tree, peering at a building some fifty yards ahead. Sunshine saw immediately that the dilapidated building was occupied. There were several horses grazing on the pasture and a thin spiral of smoke ascended from the broken-down chimneypot. Sunshine counted the horses.

'Those two moustachioed gents are there,' he said quietly, 'They're easy to pick out. But there are other horses in the corral too. I count three. That means those two gents are not alone.'

'So what do we do now?' Jordan asked.

'Well, one thing's for sure,' Sunshine said, 'we can't just blunder in and hope for the best. If Bart's being held in there that's about the worst thing we could do.'

121

Jeremiah Gibson agreed with that. 'What we do is we wait to see what's gonna happen next,' he said.

Jordan made a *tut-tut* noise. 'If we do that, Jeremiah, we might be setting down on our arses doing nothing much at all until Doomsday and we can't leave the horses back there for ever, can we?'

The boys growled in agreement. Sunshine took the point. After all, he reasoned, they didn't yet know whether Bart was being held in that ramshackle cabin, did they?

Then suddenly Fate took a hand. Slim Savage said, 'Listen, boys, I hear horses coming.'

The boys all froze and held their weapons ready.

'Don't do a thing,' Jeremiah warned. 'Just keep yourselves still and watch.'

They didn't have to wait long. Two riders rode up the trail to the cabin and dismounted. The door was opened by someone, who greeted them.

'Well, bless my belt and buttons!' Jordan Rivers exclaimed. 'Can I believe my eyes?'

Sunshine was peering between the branches and he did believe his eyes.

'Jed Cutaway and Sheriff McGiven,' he breathed.

'What in hell's name are they doing here?' Jeremiah asked in astonishment.

Sunshine grinned. 'Well, one thing's for sure. It seems Jed isn't working with his brother James at all, and the sheriff is in cahoots with Jed. Which is very interesting indeed.'

'So, this is kind of puzzling,' Jeremiah opined. 'It's kind of difficult to know what to do next.'

Sunshine was still grinning but he wasn't happy.

'Jed Cutaway and the sheriff must be here for some reason. I think we should wait for developments. Then we'll know why they're here.'

The words were hardly out of his mouth when the door of the cabin was thrust open abruptly and a whole bunch of men spilled out: Jed Cutaway, Sheriff McGiven, the two moustachioed gents and four other men, one of whom had his hands tied behind his back,

'By Jehosophat! I was right,' Jeremiah exclaimed. 'That there's Bart Bartok.'

Sunshine peered between the branches and held his Colt Peacemaker steady as the men forced Bart on to a horse. He saw that Bart Bartok was no more than a youth, quite slim and reedy, and he looked pale and terrified. Jordan pulled himself up.

'We've got the edge on them. Why don't we just rush in and free Bart? They won't know what's hit them until after it's hit them, will they?'

Sunshine shook his head.

'Hold on, I don't think we can do that, Mr Gibson. I'm wondering why Jed Cutaway and Sheriff McGiven rode up like that and why the whole bunch of them are hitting the trail so hard.'

'Well, we've left it too late, anyways,' Jeremiah Gibson said, ' 'cause they're riding off real fast like bats out of hell.'

He was right; the whole bunch were riding lickety split away from the Sheffield place as though they had forks of fire prodding their tails.

'You know what that means?' Slim Savage said. 'It means they're expecting another bunch to come riding in.'

'Well, that's real puzzling,' Gibson said. 'What d'you think we do next, Mr Shining?'

Sunshine paused for a moment, allowing his thoughts to settle into a theory.

'I guess the two Cutaway brothers are split on this. What

I've just seen tells me that Jed and his sidekicks are holding Bart, and that James Cutaway and his bullyboys have found out where Jed and the others have been holding him and they're about to strike the Sheffield place. So Jed and his boys are hightailing it pronto.'

'So what do we do?' Jordan Rivers asked.

'Well, we can't do a whole lot without our horses, can we?' Sunshine said, 'So I guess we should walk back and mount up.'

But before they could get themselves up off their butts there was a further development.

'Keep still, boys,' Jeremiah Gibson said hoarsely, 'and hold your guns ready.'

They took cover behind the trees and watched as the riders rode down the trail towards the Sheffield place.

'My Gawd! You're right, boy,' he said to Sunshine. 'That's James Cutaway and his bunch we saw on the trail back there!'

They stood among the trees and watched as James Cutaway and his men rode towards the Sheffield place. They heard James Cutaway give an order, then all his men drew rein and came to a halt.

'We're too late,' James Cutaway shouted. 'They've got clean away. All the horses have gone.'

'Why don't we take a looksee?' one of his sidekicks suggested. 'They can't have got far. Maybe they left Bart Bartok in there.'

Two of the men dismounted and ran to the cabin. The door was already swinging open.

'Nobody at home,' one of them yelled.

'Must have known we were on our way, boss,' another man shouted.

'Stop wasting time,' James Cutaway told them. 'We've gotta get on their tails. They can't be far ahead.'

The whole bunch rode off hell for leather in pursuit of Jed Cutaway and his crew.

'Well, at least we know where they're headed,' Jeremiah Gibson said. 'So what do we do?'

'We walk back for our horses and follow,' Sunshine replied.

The men had got their bits firmly between their teeth, so they hit the trail and ran. Some of them were in better condition than the others, but Sunshine outstripped them all. When they reached the horses, Gibson was breathing so hard he had to sit on a fallen tree to get his breath back.

Chingalong gave Sunshine a sidelong glance as if to say, *What happens next, you crazy man?*

'Mount up and keep together, boys,' Sunshine called. 'My guess is there's going to be gunplay ahead and we have to keep away from flying lead. As long as we rescue Bart Bartok that's all that matters.'

'Well, there's no love lost between those two brothers, that's for sure,' Jordan said.

Gibson grunted in agreement. He was still trying to recover his breath, but he could now swing on to his horse's back. When he was mounted he looked a whole lot happier.

'Now, boys, like Mr Shining says, what we have to do is rescue that boy. We don't need to get tangled up in a gun-fight, if we can avoid it.'

'That's a real pity,' Jordan said. 'I'd be more than happy to take a pot shot at either of those Cutaway boys after what they done in this part of the country.'

'Yes, but which one, that is the question?' Slim Savage asked.

CHAPTER TEN

As they rode on there was a sense of scarcely suppressed excitement. Nobody said much but they were all listening intently and wondering what would happen next. Sunshine was apprehensive. How would this bunch of hillbillies react when the chips were down? He knew Jeremiah Gibson had been in the recent war and that he could track like a native, but what would happen when the gunplay started? he wondered.

Then the shooting *did* start and the party came to an abrupt halt.

'Did I hear gunshots?' Jordan asked, somewhat over-eagerly.

Jeremiah turned his horse and held up his hand like a general addressing his troops at Gettysburg.

'Now, men, we need to play this like a hand of poker. You know what I mean? We don't just rush in like mad bulls.'

Jordan grinned. 'What are the choices, General?' he piped up.

'Well, my guess is Jed and his bunch were just waiting for Jed's brother James and his buddies to come riding along the trail.'

'Brother against brother? That don't seem hardly right,

do it?' Slim Savage said.

'Blood's a lot thinner than water when it comes to greed,' Jeremiah Gibson affirmed piously. 'Look at what happened between Cain and Abel in the Good Book.'

'Jacob and Esau too,' Slim Savage added.

There was no time for further exchanges because at that moment the shooting started in real earnest. It was unexpectedly close. Sunshine cocked his head on one side, taking in the picture. James Cutaway and his buddies were down on the trail; his brother Jed was on a slight rise to the right. Sunshine could even hear them shouting abuse at one another as they fired. But where was Bart Barkok? That was Sunshine's main concern.

'So what do we do now, General?' Jordan asked again.

'Well. . . .' Jeremiah was stroking the bristles on his chin. 'There's a slight rise just along to the right here. What we do is we keep to the high ground so we come out just above it, where we can look down and judge what to do next.'

Jordan gave a contemptuous snigger; he clearly had his own views about how they should proceed.

'OK, Mr Gibson,' Sunshine said, 'why don't you lead the way?'

Gibson led them in a wide loop away from the trail and then up a steep rise back towards the trail again. They could hear the shooting diminishing and then gaining strength again.

'OK, boys,' Gibson said. 'If we leave our horses here we can look over the edge and see what's going on. But don't look over too far in case a stray bullet comes in to take your hat off . . . or your head for that matter.'

'Which would be a danged shame for the head involved,' Jordan added with a chuckle.

They tethered their horses to stunted cottonwoods and

made their way forward, keeping low. When Sunshine peered over the crest his admiration for Jeremiah Gibson's bushcraft skills increased tenfold. They were just above the place where Jed Cutaway and his men were shooting down at Jed's brother James and *his* men. But James and his men were no longer on the trail; they were above, concealed among the trees. On the trail lay a dead horse and a man who was trying to crawl for cover.

There was no sign of Bart Bartok.

Then the shouting began. A voice roared from the trees:

'What the hell's going on here? Why are we shooting at each other like this?' Sunshine recognized James Cutaway's voice. Then Jed Cutaway spoke from immediately below him.

'We're gunning down on you because you're yellow-bellied rattlers that have no more good faith in you than the Devil himself.'

'That sounds promising,' Jordan growled. 'They'll be sending out wedding invitations next.'

Sunshine was watching the wounded man as he crawled for cover. It made him feel sick to his stomach. Then James Cutaway spoke again.

'Why can't we talk this over instead of shooting the guts out of each other? We all want the same thing, don't we?'

'Maybe we do,' Jed shouted back. 'The difference is you want to kill for it and I want to talk about it.'

James laughed; it wasn't a pleasant sound.

'Is that why you're holding that boy Bart Bartok?' he shouted.

'You don't need to worry none about him' Jed yelled back. 'We're feeding him up fine and he's as happy as a pig in shit. Ain't that so, boy?'

There was no audible reply, but Sunshine had heard

enough to judge where Bart was being held.

Now the wounded man had crawled to the edge of the trail. He raised his head and bleated like a sheep at the slaughter. Then his head dropped forward and he stopped moving.

'Well, that's one less to shoot,' Gibson muttered, somewhat unkindly.

'Another thing,' James Cutaway shouted from the trees, 'and this is for Sheriff McGiven. I guess you must have worked out by now that you're finished, boy. You might just about become the sheriff of Hades if you can stand the flames. So I hope you're ready to be burned up in those fires, 'cause that's where you're headed.'

'Sounds like war in heaven,' Slim Savage said, his knowledge of scripture being somewhat limited. Sunshine turned to Jeremiah Gibson.

'Listen, Mr Gibson, I'm going down there to rescue that boy.'

Gibson turned to him in amazement. 'You can't do that. It'll be like sticking your head in the lion's mouth.'

'Well, Mr Gibson, I figure I have to take a chance on that.'

'Are you plumb crazy, boy?'

'Maybe I am and maybe I'm not. I'd be obliged if you could cover for me, Mr Gibson, and I'd prefer not to get a bullet in my back. So pass the word along.'

Jordan chuckled again. 'You might be plumb crazy, man, but I think I'll come down there with you.'

Jeremiah Gibson almost threw up his hands in despair.

'Well, if that's what you want, I guess that's the way it has to be. If I remember right there's a kind of animal track off to the right here. If you slide down there they might not notice you until it's too late.'

Sunshine grinned. 'Thanks for the advice, Mr Gibson.

That's the way we'll go.'

Gibson stretched out his hand. 'You might be crazy, boy, but you've got *cojones*. So good luck – and call me Jerry.'

Sunshine took the offered hand and squeezed it hard.

'Thank you, Jerry.'

Sunshine and Jordan crawled to the right; sure enough there was an animal track that led down towards the trail. Generations of deer had probably been using it from time immemorial, so it was well worn. Jed Cutaway's men might have used it to outflank James Cutaway's men if they had known about it. Sunshine would have been happier on his own but Jordan had insisted on coming with him.

'OK,' Sunshine said to Jordan, 'no shooting unless it's really necessary. I want that boy out alive.'

'I'm with you,' Jordan said. 'You know something? That boy Bart knows me. He might have thought you were one of the Cutaway outfit.'

That was a point Sunshine hadn't considered.

'OK,' he said. 'Let's go.'

As they crept down the animal track there was a sudden outbreak of shooting and cursing, mainly from the James Cutaway side. *Bethany Bartok's land must be awful precious if brothers will fight to the death over it,* Sunshine thought to himself. He hadn't got more than halfway down the animal track before Jordan suddenly touched him on the back.

'Stop where you are!' he hissed.

Sunshine stopped and looked back at Jordan. Jordan mouthed at him and jerked his thumb over to the right. Sunshine froze and listened. He heard rustling to the right of the track. James Cutaway's men might not know about the animal track but some of them were crawling towards it from the right, hoping to enfilade the enemy. The sudden outbreak of shooting had been a diversion.

Before Sunshine had time to realize what that implied the foliage to the right of the track parted and a revolver poked out, followed by the face of a man. The man saw the track and smiled. He looked to the right, where James Cutaway's men were firing, then to the left, where he came face to face with Sunshine and his Colt Peacemaker.

Sunshine could have shot the man through the eye; instead he brought the Peacemaker down on the man's head. The man rolled over sideways and fired his gun. The bullet went harmlessly into the air.

Before Sunshine could stop to think another man reared up; his gun was pointed directly at him. *Hell's bells!* Sunshine thought, *I'm going to die.* But before the man could pull the trigger there was a flash; the gunman reared back and fell.

'Thank Gawd for that!' Jordan said from behind Sunshine. Sunshine saw that the man was gasping for breath.

Sunshine spun round to the right, but there were no more intruders. There was no time to think about that, though, since James Cutaway's men were running across the trail, firing as they came. Jed Cutaway's men were firing back at them with equal ferocity.

'My Gawd! All hell's breaking out,' Jordan said. 'What do we do now?'

Sunshine wasn't sure how to respond. He raised his head just enough to see what was happening on the trail.

'Keep your head down,' Jordan warned.

Jed Cutaway's men were busy firing down at the trail; Sunshine saw two men fall as they rushed forward. *My God! This is a massacre,* he thought.

Then another idea occurred to him. This might be just the chance he needed to rescue that boy.

'Cover for me,' he said to Jordan.

'I've been covering for you,' Jordan hissed. 'Are you utterly off your head, man?'

Sunshine pushed his way off the side of the track and wriggled forward. As he did so a bullet slashed through the grass just beyond him. Another lucky escape!

He could hear the shooting just ahead, but where were they? Then suddenly he saw Jed Cutaway. Cutaway was too busy firing at the *hombre* below to notice Sunshine crawling up on him. But where was Bart Bartok?

Then Jed Cutaway must have seen someone just beyond Sunshine's vision to the right. He turned. There was moment of suspense as Jed saw Sunshine and recognized him. First fear, then astonishment, then fury appeared on his face. Then he swung his Winchester round. But a Winchester is more cumbersome than a Colt Peacemaker and Sunshine got his shot in first.

Jed Cutaway took the shot high in the chest. A forty-five bullet can knock a man right back, but a curious thing happened: Jed Cutaway jolted sideways, then reared right up as though he intended to run forward towards the trail. Then he caught two shots in quick succession from the men below, one in the neck and one in the head. He jerked and fell back with blood spurting from his head.

'Well, I'll be damned!' Jordan shouted. 'You damned killed Jed Cutaway!'

Sunshine wanted to reply but his lips were frozen and he fell forward on to his face.

'My God, you've been hit!' Jordan shouted.

Sunshine rolled over on to his back. 'I can't feel a thing,' he said.

*

Then something remarkable happened. Someone from Jed Cutaway's side roared out:

'The boss has been killed.'

Then another man a little further off shouted:

'You've killed Jed Cutaway.'

Suddenly the shooting stopped. It was as though a thunderbolt had struck the earth.

'What?' came another shout. 'You mean Jed Cutaway has been killed?'

'Dead as a nail,' someone yelled from Jed Cutaway's side. Then there was a great murmuring.

'I'm getting out of here!' yet another voice cried out.

Sunshine looked up and saw that the men from Jed Cutaway's side were moving as fast as they could away from the action. Then he looked below and saw that the James Cutaway boys were pulling out too.

'My Gawd! You did it,' Jordan said. 'You done killed Jed Cutaway and you're clean and alive.' He knelt over Sunshine and examined him. 'Get up. You haven't been hit, man. It was just the shock.' He reached down and heaved Sunshine up. 'You're clean, man. You're good and clean.'

Sunshine didn't feel clean. He felt like vomiting.

Then they heard the sound of horses whinnying and men shouting.

'They're riding away,' someone said. 'Leaving us to bury the dead.' It was Jeremiah Gibson and he was smiling triumphantly.

'You see what happened?' Jordan said. 'This young guy killed Jed Cutaway.'

'Is that so?' Gibson replied. Sunshine struggled to recover his balance, determined not to vomit.

'Have you found Bart Bartok?' he asked.

'Over here,' Slim Savage said.

Sunshine realized he was still clutching the Colt Peacemaker. He thrust it into its holster and staggered forward to meet Bart Barkok.

'So you're Bart Bartok?' he said.

The boy didn't know whether to laugh or cry. 'Am I free now?' he asked.

'Free as you'll ever be,' Slim Savage assured him.

'So, what's the score?' Jordan asked.

'Well, this ain't exactly a chess game,' Gibson told him. 'but the score's more or less even, Three dead on this side, including Jed Cutaway, and four on the other side . . . and one horse, if you count horses.'

'All because of a slice of land that ain't worth two bits,' Slim Savage added.

'I reckon you're wrong there,' Gibson said. 'But we won't know till they start drilling, will we?'

'What do we do with the dead men?' Jordan asked.

'Well, we can't leave them out here for the coyotes and the buzzards to peck at. So I guess we load them on the backs of horses and take them into town for decent burial.'

Sunshine was feeling a little steadier now.

'Your ma will sure be glad to see you,' he said to Bart. 'Did they treat you badly?'

Bart was still trembling so much that they threw a blanket over his shoulders.

'No, they didn't treat me bad; they just threatened to kill me if my ma didn't sign over the land.'

'Well, you can stop worrying about that now,' Sunshine told him.

He went to look at the corpses. Jed Cutaway, who'd been hit in the head was a truly grisly sight. Then Sunshine looked at the face of the more heavily mousta-chioed *hombre*; his moustache was now decidedly droopy.

He had a look of astonishment on his dead face, as though he couldn't believe he had been hit.

They rounded up the horses that had been abandoned and hoisted the corpses across their backs with due respect.

Sunshine went up to where Chingalong was feeding on the sparse grass on the other side of the bluff.

'Well, Ching,' he said, 'I guess you heard all that shenanigans. And I'm glad you weren't unduly bothered by it.'

Chingalong looked at Sunshine and snorted.

'That's my boy,' Sunshine said, patting him on the head.

They rode back to the main trail more solemnly than triumphantly. There was no sign of the survivors from either side. It seemed that the death of Jed Cutaway had hit both sides like an avalanche of boulders. When they reached the trail Jeremiah Gibson brought the party to a halt in his usual commanding fashion.

'Well, men,' he said, 'I think this is where we part company.' He looked at Bart Bartok. 'I think you should go back to the farm and help your ma to rejoice at your homecoming.'

'Like the Prodigal Son in the Good Book,' Slim Savage added piously.

Jeremiah looked at Sunshine. 'You should go with him, son. We'll ferry these dead stiffs back to town.'

'And give the Funeral Director the good news,' Slim Savage said mournfully.

'And by the way, son,' Gibson said to Sunshine, 'I'd like to thank you for doing a great job with that Colt Peacemaker of yourn.' He stretched out his large paw and gave Sunshine's hand a firm squeeze.

Then Jeremiah Gibson, Jordan Rivers, Slim Savage, and the other close-mouthed *hombre* set off along the trail towards town with a grim procession of dead men draped across the backs of horses. It was a somewhat dispiriting sight.

Bart Bartok looked at Sunshine and smiled for the first time.

'I don't know who you are, Mr Shining, but I believe you saved my life, and I must thank you for that.'

Sunshine smiled back. 'Well, your ma and your sister will be glad to see you and that's all that matters, isn't it?'

'How come you got tangled up in this mess?' the young man asked.

Sunshine told him how he had come upon the homestead by chance, had fired a couple of rounds to frighten off the gunmen, and how he had stayed on to help Bethany Bartok around the farm.

'Well, like Mr Slim Savage said, I'm like the Prodigal Son and I'm not too proud of that.'

'I think you should say that to your ma,' Sunshine said. 'As I understand it, it's too late to talk to your pa about it.'

'I can make up for it on the farm,' the boy said.

'Well, your ma needs all the help she can get,' Sunshine agreed.

When they reached the homestead Berthany Bartok and Elspeth were driving the cows in for milking. There wasn't a lot of driving needed; the cows just ambled along to the milking shed to ease their load of milk. When Bethany looked up she stared hard at Sunshine and Bart, as though she was seeing some kind of heavenly vision.

'My God! You're back,' she cried. Then she ran to the horse and hugged the boy's knee. Bart looked suitably embarrassed. Then he jumped down from the horse and submitted to her embraces. Elspeth just looked at Sunshine and smiled.

'So you're back safe,' she said.

'He shot Jed Cutaway,' Bart said. 'That's why I'm free.'

'So you shot Jed Cutaway?' Elspeth asked in astonishment.

'He was about to shoot me,' Sunshine said. 'Then his brother James – or one of his sidekicks – shot him in the head.'

'I don't understand,' Elspeth said. 'You mean the brothers Cutaway were shooting at one another?'

Bart Bartok suddenly shook himself right back to life. He told his mother and Elspeth about the shoot-out in graphic detail, even with certain embellishments about how he had just been about to make a break for it when Fate intervened in the shape of Jeremiah Gibson, Sunshine, and the others.

Then he told them how he had been taken prisoner by Jed Cutaway and his men and held in the most terrible conditions. Yes, he had been held at Stinking Flats, then moved on to the Sullivan place.

'They kept me tied up most of the time,' he said, and his lips trembled as he spoke about it.

'Well, you're safe now,' his mother assured him, 'and it's time to feed you up.'

Yes, it was time to eat and Bart lost no time in devouring all the food available.

This kid sure likes to eat, Sunshine thought to himself. *Those kidnappers must have kept him half-starved. I guess he's been spoiled rotten by his doting ma in the past.*

'Now, I gonna hit the hay and take a long, long nap,' the boy announced.

'The boy's been through hell and high water and back,' Bethany said after Bart had left them.

'He could have been killed,' Elspeth said, none too sympathetically.

'Well, thank the Lord, it's over now,' Bethany said.

'Are you sure it's over?' Elspeth asked her sharply. She looked at Sunshine for support. 'Is it really over?' she asked him. Sunshine shook his head.

'I don't know when over is over,' he said. 'Every ending is a new beginning. That's the way life swings along.'

'What exactly does that mean?' Elspeth asked him.

'I guess it means just what James Cutaway wants it to mean.'

'How d'you figure that out?' Bethany asked.

'Well. . . .' Sunshine tilted his head to one side, 'what I think I mean is: there's a whole lot of unanswered questions floating around here.'

Elspeth raised an attractive eyebrow.

'Such as?'

'Such as how does James Cutaway feel about the death of his brother? Why were those boys at war with one another? What did their kin feel about it? Why were they keen enough on getting their hands on your patch of land to kidnap your son and shoot at one another over it?'

'That's one hell of a lot of questions,' Bethany said.

'Sure,' he agreed, 'and I guess things aren't going to be put to rest until we find the answers.'

'How do we do that?' Elspeth asked.

Sunshine shrugged. 'Come morning I'm going to ride into town and look around.'

'You mean like lift a few stones and look underneath to

see what you find?' Bethany said in astonishment.

Sunshine smiled. 'Well, that's quite a good way of putting it, Bethany. Men have been known to turn over stones and find gold, you know.'

'That's if you believe in fairy tales,' Elspeth countered.

Sunshine gave her a long warm smile.

'Well, I believe them if you do,' he said.

Bethany was shaking her head.

'You must be crazy,' she said. 'You don't know what you might find in town, do you?'

Elspeth was smiling to herself. 'Well, Mr Shining, I'll tell you something: if you're going into town I'm going with you.'

Bethany was about to put her foot down, but she restrained herself.

'Well, I guess I can't stop you. But make sure you take guns with you in case of trouble, you hear me?'

CHAPTER ELEVEN

'It would be a whole lot better if you stayed on the farm and helped your ma out,' Sunshine said to Elspeth when they were at breakfast next morning. 'This whole business is wearing her out.'

'Ma is a whole lot tougher than you think,' Elspeth replied. 'I'm going with you. Remember what happened last time. That dumb sheriff was about to throw you into the town jail but I flapped my eyes at him and he forgot about it.'

'Well, I must admit that did help some,' he agreed. Elspeth was wearing her working clothes instead of her fine city duds, but to Sunshine she looked even more attractive.

'I shall ride into town on Felicity,' Elspeth went on. 'She's a fine mare and she won't give us any trouble.'

'Just as long as Chingalong doesn't have a yen for her,' Sunshine mused.

If Elspeth blushed Sunshine didn't see it since at that point she was sliding a Winchester carbine into the saddle holster.

They hit the trail and headed towards town.

'So you shot Jed Cutaway,' Elspeth said.

'Like I said, I had to, but I didn't want to. When I looked down at his dead face it made me sick to my stomach.

Something tells me I'm not cut out to be a gunslinger.'

She glanced at him sideways.

'You're far too good for that, Mr Shining.'

He smiled. 'You think so, Miss Bartok?'

'I really do.' She smiled too, but to herself. 'So what will you do when this ugly business is over?'

'I'm not good at making plans, Miss Elspeth. I think I'll wait and see where the tides of Fate roll me.'

'So you believe in Fate, Mr Shining?'

'Fate or Destiny,' he said, 'depends on how you look at it. I guess I'm not cut out to be a farm boy either. So I might just move right on.'

'That could be . . . further West or back East. . . ?' She was still smiling to herself.

'It might depend on . . . things.'

'What sort of things?'

They were now riding side by side, so close that their knees were rubbing together. She glanced at him and smiled. It was a sweet and modest smile and for a moment he was tongue-tied. Then he leaned towards her and kissed her on the mouth. Her lips tasted as sweet as the sweetest honey he had ever tasted. It was like all the bees in the world had come together to produce it!

After they had broken away they rode on in amazement for a while. Sunshine felt so ecstatic he thought he might fall right out of the saddle.

'And what do you plan to do?' he asked her when he had recovered his breath. She raised an eyebrow.

'That depends on a lot of things too, Mr Shining.'

They stared at one another and it was as though the sun was shining through the trees on the first day of Creation.

'Like what?' he almost whispered.

For a moment all she did was smile. Then she looked down the trail towards town.

'That might depend on you, Mr Shining,' she said, so quietly that he barely heard her. Then he took another deep breath.

'D'you mind if I ask you a question?' he said.

She gave him another irresistible smile and his heart seemed to turn right over in his chest.

'D'you think we make a good team, Miss Elspeth?'

She gave a quiet murmur of laughter.

'What sort of question is that, Mr Shining? After all we're not horses, are we?'

What a damned clumsy fool I am! he thought. 'What I mean,' he stammered, 'is, d'you think you could marry me, Miss Elspeth?'

She looked startled, but not unduly surprised.

'What kind of proposal is that, Mr Shining?'

Sunshine wondered what to do next. After all, a man on a horse can't get down on his knees, can he? He looked at her for a moment and saw a wonderful look of anticipation in her eyes. He reached out and took her hand.

'I have nothing to offer you except my love, Elspeth, but will you please marry me?'

They looked at one another and it seemed as though the sun had now risen above the trees and was shining with full radiancy.

'I believe I will,' she said. 'I believe I will.'

They leaned over and kissed again while the horses kept jogging on towards town.

When they reached town there was a kind of haze hanging over the place. It was more psychological than physical, as though even the houses themselves were in mourning.

'Where are we going?' Elspeth asked him.

'Maybe we should call in on the store and drink a mug of Mrs Snaze's good strong coffee. Then I'd like to look in at the "Close Shave, We Do You Good".'

'You think you need a shave?' she queried.

'I think I'm going to be a little too busy for that. I want to consult the funeral directing part of the firm.'

'You mean Stan Baldock and partners?' she said.

'Well now. . . .' Sunshine grinned. 'So my barber's got a name, has he?'

They dismounted and tethered their mounts to the hitching rail outside the general store. Both horses immediately dipped their noses into the drinking trough where Slam Smith had taken his last bath.

'My my! Miss Elspeth and Mr Shining,' the storekeeper greeted as they entered the store. 'What can I do for you on this happy day?'

'We've just looked in to see how the town's rolling along,' Sunshine told him.

'Well, the town's in an unholy mess right now,' the storekeeper said. 'Mr Baldock is run off his feet with all the dead they brought in yesterday. He'll be sawing and planing for a couple of days before he can tuck those stiffs down in their final resting places.' He looked at Sunshine. 'They tell me you shot Jed Cutaway.'

'Mr Shining freed my brother,' Elspeth told him.

'Well, that's a relief, anyway,' the storekeeper said. 'Your ma will be pleased about that.'

At that moment Mrs Snaze appeared.

'Why don't you come through for a coffee?' she invited. Sunshine thought she looked a trifle on edge.

They went through and sat at a table where Mrs Snaze served the good strong brew.

'Things are pretty quiet in town today,' Sunshine observed.

'That's because folks are keeping to their homes,' Mrs

143

Snaze told him. 'Everyone's talking about what happened between the Cutaway brothers and their men.'

'And everyone's talking about you too, Mr Shining,' Mr Snaze put in. He was enjoying a coffee with them since trade was so dead.

'They must be putting together a pack of lies,' Sunshine suggested.

'What are they saying?' Elspeth asked Snaze.

'They're saying Mr Shining came face to face with Jed Cutaway, outdrew him and shot him down to free your brother Bart. They say Mr Shining is a top gunfighter with a charmed life.'

'Well, that's a slight exaggeration, Mr Snaze,' Sunshine said. 'I just did what I had to do in the circumstances, and I got lucky, that's all.'

'Well, you know how folks talk. So you'd better watch your step in case you walk right into a pile of horse shit.'

Sunshine shrugged. 'I'll bear that in mind, Mr Snaze.' He got up from the table.

'Where are you going?' Elspeth asked him.

'I'm just going to take a stroll down to the Close Shave, We Do You Good,' Sunshine said.

'I think you'll find Stan Baldock is closed for business at the moment due to overwork in the other department,' the storekeeper told him.

'I'm coming with you,' Elspeth announced with determination.

'No,' Sunshine said firmly. 'You stay here and enjoy this good coffee.'

Mrs Snaze looked amazed.

'My, oh my,' she said. 'You talk like an old married couple.'

Sunshine looked at Elspeth and they both laughed.

*

Sunshine stepped out on to Main Street and looked both ways. There was scarcely a soul in sight. He walked down to the Close Shave and saw the sign on the door. *Closed for shaving and haircutting owing to pressure of work.*

He was about to turn away when the door swung open and Stan Baldock beckoned him in.

'Get yourself in quickly,' the barber hissed. 'Don't you know you're a marked man?'

Sunshine went inside and Baldock pulled down the blinds.

A marked man! Sunshine thought. *That sounds like a board for target practice.* He sat down in the barber's chair.

'Don't sit there,' the barber shouted. 'Someone might shoot through the window and take you out. I've got enough dead men to put in the ground and I don't want any more.'

'So where would you like me to sit?'

Baldock beckoned again. 'Come through to the back where we can talk.'

Sunshine walked through to the back room and sat down in an over-stuffed chair.

'What's this about being a marked man?' he asked the barber. Stan Baldock sat down opposite him.

'Well, people are all talking about how you killed Jed Cutaway in the battle out there.'

'I don't think I killed him,' Sunshine objected. 'I think one of his brother's men killed him.'

'That's the trouble when brothers go head to head. Others get caught between them like flies and get themselves squashed.'

'That sounds a little on the grim side,' Sunshine said. It occurred to him that he was in even more danger than he had feared – and maybe Elspeth was too.

'I guess I should go back and warn Elspeth,' he said.

Before he could push himself up from the chair there sounded a rumpus from the back and a woman came rushing into the room.

'Stan! Stan!' she cried, 'Something terrible's happening out there in the back alley.' She stared bug-eyed at Sunshine. The barber grabbed her by the arms.

'Don't fret, my dear. This is Mr Shining, the man who killed Jed Cutaway.'

That didn't do much to reassure his wife. In fact, if anything she looked even more white-faced.

'You shouldn't be here, sir. That James Cutaway is a terrible man. He's shouting about how he wants you dead for killing his brother.'

'Oh, my Gawd!' Stan Baldock said. 'He probably knows you're in here. What are we gonna do?'

'Well, there's only one thing to do,' Sunshine said. 'I've got to get out of here for your safety.'

He went through to the front again and peered out between the blinds. Main Street appeared to be deserted.

'It's all happening somewhere out back,' Mrs Baldock said from behind him. Sunshine turned to Stan Baldock.

'Sorry I bothered you, Mr Baldock. I'll just go out on to Main Street. I want you to bolt the door behind me. There's no reason why you good people should be involved in this.'

He unbolted the door and stepped out on to Main Street.

He heard shooting from somewhere behind him. He drew the Colt Peacemaker and checked it. Then he walked along the sidewalk towards the store, keeping as close as possible to the buildings. He could see Chingalong and Elspeth's horse. Now they weren't drinking at the trough. They were just standing slightly apart as though deep in conversation. For some reason Sunshine found that reassuring. All he had to do now was walk to the store and warn Elspeth to get out of town.

Before he could take another step the door of the store opened and Elspeth appeared with Mrs Snaze, as if by thought transference. They turned towards him in astonishment. Now he had to step down off the sidewalk and cross the gap between the two buildings. As he stepped off the sidewalk he heard the sound of approaching feet; suddenly a man came round the corner of the building. It was Sheriff McGiven. He was holding a shooter in his right hand.

'So, it's you!' the sheriff gasped.

Sunshine could see Elspeth and Mrs Snaze standing behind McGiven; he knew that if he fired the Colt he might accidentally hit one of them. So he raised his gun to shoulder level.

McGiven looked momentarily bewildered. He pointed his gun at Sunshine, as though he was about to shoot, but Fate intervened and he never pulled the trigger. A shot came from behind the buildings, the sheriff jerked forward and fell on to his face.

Mrs Snaze screamed.

'Get back inside!' Sunshine shouted, but Elspeth was already bundling Mrs Snaze back into the store.

Sunshine ran back to the sidewalk and pressed himself against the wall of the building. The next moment another man appeared: it was James Cutaway. Cutaway rushed forward and looked down at McGiven's body.

'Why, you yellow-bellied skunk!' he shouted. Then he stood right over McGiven and fired two shots into his body. McGiven didn't even jerk; he was already dead.

James Cutaway turned and saw Sunshine standing in

the shadows on the sidewalk. Both men pulled their triggers simultaneously but only one gun fired. James Cutaway fell back against the sidewalk and stared at his revolver in dismay. He tried to struggle to his feet but he fell forward right across the body of Sheriff McGiven.

Sunshine looked down at the Colt Peacemaker in his hand; the barrel was still smoking.

'My God! I've killed him,' he said.

There was a moment of deathly silence, then Main Street sprang to life. People came running from every door to look in astonishment at the two dead men.

'You've killed James Cutaway,' someone said.

Sunshine was still looking down at the Colt Peacemaker as though it were a rattlesnake that had just raised its head and struck. He became aware of someone standing beside him.

'You killed them,' Stan Baldock said. Sunshine didn't reply. He just held out the gun.

'Here, take this before it kills someone else.'

Stan Baldock shook his head.

'No, sir, you might need it. Just put it back in its holster.'

Sunshine slid the gun into its holster. When he looked up he saw Elspeth walking towards him. She must have seen the look of horror on his face for she ran straight up to him and put her arms around him.

'I saw what happened. James Cutaway tried to kill you. Thank God he didn't succeed!' Apparently, after bundling Mrs Snaze into the store she had opened the door, looked out and seen everything.

One of the men knelt down and retrieved James Cutaway's gun. He spun the chambers; they were full of empty shell cases.

'He tried to gun down on you but he'd used the last two bullets on the sheriff,' he told Sunshine. Someone gave a grim laugh.

'So he sort of killed himself.'

Someone clapped Sunshine on the back. 'You're a lucky son-of-a-gun.'

'Well, that's the end of those two brothers in blood,' another man said. 'Now they can wreak mayhem in the other place.'

'Wherever that might be,' someone said, and laughed.

'Two more stiffs to bury.' Stan Baldock sighed.

'That's money in the till,' the same man rejoined. 'You'll soon be as rich as that Greek guy with money coming out of his ears.'

The storekeeper had now appeared in his blue-and-white striped apron.

'Come into the store,' he said to Sunshine. 'You need something a lot stronger than coffee to set you up.'

Sunshine didn't dispute that. He took Elspeth's arm and they walked to the store together. As they approached the door a cheer went up from the crowd.

'You're a hero,' the storekeeper told him.

They went inside and through to the back room where Snaze produced a glass of the best rye whiskey.

'Here, get this down. You've earned it.'

Sunshine was shaking. He sat down and took a gulp of whiskey. It nearly took the top of his head off but it calmed him down considerably. *What's happened to me?* he wondered. Elspeth reached across and took his hand.

'I thought I might lose you,' she said.

'Just after I'd found you, too' he said, somewhat inconsequentially. Outside they could hear the sound of folk laughing and cheering. Snaze grinned.

'They're celebrating the end of an era,' he said.

*

149

'Time to go home,' Elspeth told Sunshine.

'Time to go home,' Sunshine agreed. They went out and mounted their horses. Sunshine patted Chingalong's neck.

'Well, Ching, what did you make of that bust-up?'

Chingalong tossed his head and Felicity gave a low snort.

'I think they both agree you're lucky to be alive, and I'm a lot more than lucky,' Elspeth said. 'You're still alive and we're together.' She leaned across and kissed him.

Though he was shaking he felt a whole lot better.

They rode back slowly. Elspeth was humming quietly to herself.

'What are you thinking?' he asked her.

'I'm thinking of the future,' she said.

'What do you see ahead?'

She turned and smiled.

'I see a road. It's kind of bumpy in places but there's smooth patches too,' she paused, 'and I see trees with the sun shining brightly between them.'

'That sounds like a very pretty picture.'

'Maybe you should paint it, Mr Shining.'

Sunshine thought on that for a moment.

'I have a better idea, Miss Bartok. Instead of painting it I think I'm going to live it.'

When they reached the farmstead Bethany was working hard as usual. Bart was lounging back in a rocking chair on the veranda. As soon as he heard them approaching he sprang to life and headed for the door. He was obviously jittery after his incarceration. Then he turned and shaded his eyes against the sun and relaxed.

'So you're back,' he crowed.

'So we're back,' Elspeth said with a tinge of irony.

They dismounted and took their horses into the corral where they could feed and drink their fill.

'You've done a real good job today,' Sunshine told Chingalong. 'You've seen more things than I care to mention. You carry on like this and you'll have a whole store of things to tell future generations.'

Bethany appeared.

'Good to see you back safe,' she said. 'I hope everything went according to plan.' She put her arms round Elspeth and kissed her on both cheeks. Then she turned to Sunshine. 'You look somewhat washed out,' she said, 'You'd better come right inside and tell me what happened in town.'

They went into the cabin and sat at the table; after a moment Bart came in to join them.

'What happened, as it turned out, was quite a lot,' Elspeth said.

'A lot of what?' Bart enquired.

'Well,' Elspeth said. 'Two men got killed. One of them was the sheriff and the other one was James Cutaway himself.'

Bethany was halfway through loading her stubby pipe. She stared at Elspeth in astonishment.

'You mean James Cutaway is dead?' she asked in wonder. 'How come?' Elspeth wasn't one for mincing words.

'Sunshine shot him – in self-defence,' she said.

Bethany stared at Sunshine.

'You shot James Cutaway?'

Sunshine's face was glowing with embarrassment. and something like shame.

'He was about to shoot me, so I just pulled the trigger. I was lucky. I didn't know he was out of bullets.'

'Because he'd just used the last two bullets shooting the dead sheriff,' Elspeth added.

Then she laughed and broke down in tears of relief.

'What happened to all the other gunmen?' Bart asked.

'We don't know,' Sunshine said. 'They've probably abandoned ship, like the rats they are.'

Elspeth was smiling through her tears. 'We've got something else to tell you.'

Bethany had now succeeded in lighting her pipe. She puffed out a cloud of blue smoke.

'So, what the hell!' she said. 'Did the sun fall down from the sky?'

'No,' Elspeth said joyfully, 'it's a whole lot worse than that. Mr Shining asked me to marry him.'

Bethany clamped her teeth on her stubby pipe and looked thoughtful. Then she took the pipe out of her mouth and held it up like an Indian chief summoning the ancestors.

'Did you say yes?'

Sunshine was smiling nervously.

'I did intend to ask for your approval, Mrs Bartok, but it sort of crept up on us.'

Bethany grinned and nodded.

'And how will you support my daughter, Mr Shining?'

Sunshine swallowed hard.

'I'm not sure I know the answer to that, Mrs Bartok.'

Bethany nodded. 'So she did say yes?'

'Indeed she did.'

Bethany raised both arms.

'Then there's no more to be said, is there?'

In fact there was quite a lot more to be said, though not on that subject directly. At sunup next morning they all took an early breakfast, except for Bart who was still snoring in bed. Sunshine realized that the boy wasn't too keen on work.

There was hay to reap. Sunshine took the scythe, sharpened it up and started swinging it in the long grass. Elspeth followed, piling it up in stoops. The weather was fine but there were darkening clouds in the west, suggesting a coming storm.

'The sooner we get this under cover the better,' Bethany said.

As she spoke Sunshine looked up and saw riders approaching over the brow of the hill. He wasn't wearing the gunbelt, so he wondered what he should do.

'It's OK,' Bethany said. 'I see who it is. It's my neighbour Jeremiah Gibson and the boys.'

As they rode closer Sunshine saw that it was indeed Jeremiah Gibson. With him were Jordan Rivers, Slim Savage, and Jon Jenson. They rode right up to Sunshine and Elspeth. Jeremiah Gibson acted as spokesman as usual.

'Good morning, Bethany,' he said. 'Me and the boys have come to help out. We reckon you need it.' He looked at Sunshine and grinned. 'You deserve it, too, Mr Shining, after what you did.'

'You sure do,' echoed Jordan Rivers.

They all got down from their horses and tethered them at the edge of the hayfield. They were all carrying reaping hooks. Those boys knew how to work: they had the hay stored in the barn in practically no time at all. Then they went to the house, where Bethany produced some of her best brew and they proceeded to get a little tipsy. They were all laughing and joking when they heard a commotion outside. Then someone rapped smartly on the door.

'Who's there?' Bethany shouted.

'It's the law,' a peremptory voice replied. The door swung open to reveal a tall rugged man wearing a badge of office on his chest.

'Why, good day to you, Marshal,' Jeremiah Gibson

greeted cheerfully.

'Please step inside, Marshal.' Bethany stepped back from the door to allow the man admittance. The marshal stepped inside and looked at her rosy face.

'Which one of you is Mr Shining?' he asked. Since he had probably met most of the others before it seemed a strange question, especially since he was looking directly at Sunshine. Sunshine held up his hand.

'That's me, Marshal.'

The marshal stepped closer to Sunshine and looked him in the eye. He had an unflinching gaze, enough to frighten the pants off a bullfrog.

'So you're the man who killed the Cutaway brothers,' he said. Sunshine bowed his head.

'Well, not exactly, Marshal.'

'Not at all,' Jordan Rivers piped up. 'That was one of James Cutaway's bunch. I seed it myself.'

'That's the truth,' Jeremiah Gibson affirmed. 'We were trying to rescue Bart Bartok. We succeeded, too.'

'I saw what happened to James Cutaway,' Elspeth said. 'James Cutaway had just shot Sheriff McGiven, then he turned his gun on Mr Shining and Mr Shining shot him in self-defence.' Elspeth could hardly get her words out, she was so overcome by the memory of that scene. The marshal turned his attention on Sunshine.

'Those Cutaways left wives and children. You might not know that, Mr Shining.'

'I guessed that might be so,' Sunshine admitted.

At last the marshal's grim face broke into a smile.

'You know those Cutaways were once the richest ranchers for miles around here. Old man Cutaway and his father before him were the wealthiest men in the county, but they let their money run through their hands like water. Now it's all gone back into the ground.'

Bethany took out her pipe and spoke.

'That's why those boys wanted to get their hands on my land. They thought it would make them rich again.'

'That's likely the truth, Mrs Bartok,' the marshal said.

'And that's why those brothers came to shooting at each other. They both wanted the whole of the pie instead of just a share.'

The marshal nodded solemnly.

'Each wanted to be king of the castle, Mrs Bartok.' He turned to Sunshine again. 'There'll have to be a hearing on this, Mr Shining. I guess you know that. I'll need to talk to the judge about it.'

'Well, I'll be here whenever you need me,' Sunshine said.

After the marshal had ridden away nobody spoke for some minutes. Then Jeremiah Gibson piped up again.

'Well, there's a lot of long faces around here, but I want you all to remember that shindig I invited you all to come to on Saturday. Me and my lady will be looking forward to greeting you all. So don't let her down, because she can't abide being disappointed!'

That gave rise to loud guffaws of laughter. Everyone knew Eveline Gibson was cut in the old frontier jib, tough as hickory on the outside and soft as new butter under the skin.

The shindig wasn't disappointing either. Jeremiah Gibson had invited a few local farmers who could play the fiddle and squeeze the squeezebox or beat out a passable rhythm on an old tin drum. They weren't too tuneful but they scraped and squeezed away in time with the old tin drum and everyone enjoyed the dance. Sunshine and Elspeth were prancing around together and really enjoying it.

'Well, I'll be damned!' Sunshine said to Elspeth, 'I

didn't know I could dance so well.'

'I've got news for you, Sunshine,' she whispered back, 'You've got a few things to learn in that department.'

Sunshine chuckled and thought to himself, *Sure, and I've got a lot to learn in some other departments, too.*

Suddenly the band stopped playing and Jeremiah Gibson called everyone to order.

'Now listen up, folks. Our good friend and neighbour Mrs Bethany Bartok here has something to say.' He stepped aside and Bethany Bartok took his place. For once she didn't have her stubby pipe in her mouth.

'Well, good folks and neighbours, I have an announcement to make.' She gave an eloquent flourish of her hand. 'My daughter Elspeth, who as you all know has just got back from the East—'

'We know that,' Jordan Rivers shouted.

'Get on with the announcement,' Eveline Gibson piped up.

'OK, OK,' Bethany retorted. 'I just wanted to say Elspeth and Mr Shining have decided to—'

'Hitch up together,' someone suggested.

'Well, what I mean is. . . .' Bethany left a significant pause. 'Well, what I mean is . . . they aim to get married,' she finished in a rush.

There was a momentary silence, then everyone cheered and stamped on the floor.

'Strike up the band,' Jeremiah Gibson shouted.

Those so-called musicians might not have been top-notch, but they made up for any shortcomings with their enthusiasm, and soon they were scraping and squeezing and banging away like the beginning of the world had come. Even Bart joined in the dancing like a man whose joints were in peak condition.

In the interval, when everyone was sitting down and

enjoying some good strong liquor, Bart suddenly appeared before Sunshine and grasped his hand.

'So, you're gonna marry my sister,' he said. 'I'm right glad about that.' Then he started pumping Sunshine's hand up and down so hard it was fit to come off. 'And I've got to thank you for rescuing me from those killers.' He raised his eyebrows. 'They would have killed me, you know.' He held up a handsome gold watch. 'Lookee here. I got my watch back, too.'

Sunshine was pleased about the watch but he was even gladder when the band struck up and everyone started to dance again.

Next morning Sunshine and Elspeth were sitting at table enjoying their breakfast of flapjacks and honey and beans when Bethany spoke again; this time she did have her stubby pipe in her hand.

'I've been thinking about the future,' she said. 'Not my future but yours.'

'But Ma, you've got a future too,' Elspeth protested.

Bart said nothing; he was still sleeping off the effects of his gyrations and an excess of strong booze. Bethany raised an eyebrow.

'My future isn't important. It's your future that counts.' She tapped with nervous fingers on the table. 'I see now, I've been damned selfish.'

'How so?' Elspeth asked her. 'I'm the one who's been selfish, leaving you and going East like that with those horrible people.'

'Well,' Bethany said, 'I guess we're all selfish at times. That's what human nature is like.' She shrugged her shoulders. 'What I wanted to say is, I wanted to keep the farm going for your pa's sake. He had worked so hard to keep it together and he was a good man, so I felt obliged for his sake. . . .' she paused to swallow hard . . . 'to keep this farm in the family.'

'We all appreciate that, Ma,' Elspeth said quietly.

'Sure you do,' Bethany agreed. 'But that's not all I have to say.' She wrinkled her brow in thought. 'I've been think-ing about that part of land we call "the Badlands". I had a dream last night.'

'A dream?' Elspeth echoed.

'Yes, I do dream,' Bethany said. 'I know you think that I'm a crazy old woman who's gone completely off her rocker.'

'Why don't you tell us about the dream, Mrs Bartok?' Sunshine said.

Bethany smiled. 'In this dream my husband came to me just as plain as I see you. Then he spoke.'

'What did he say?' Sunshine asked. Bethany was still smiling wistfully.

'He told me about the farm and the Badlands. He said: "Don't fret about that, Bethany. You can keep the whole farm. You don't need to sell off anything to anyone. But, if you want to hold everything together, you have to agree to have the Badlands developed because there's oil under the earth there and it's worth a mint of money.'

'You mean Pa said all that to you?' Elspeth exclaimed.

Bethany nodded. 'That's what he said. Of course, I don't know whether it was him or whether it was me talking to myself in my sleep. But it was real to me.'

Sunshine and Elspeth looked at one another in amaze-ment.

'Well,' Sunshine said, 'it doesn't matter one way or the other, does it? As long as your dream is telling you the truth.'

Bethany gave him a sidelong glance.

'You've got a good head on your shoulders, boy, and that's what we need in this family.'

'So what are you going to do?' Elspeth asked her.

'I'm gonna get myself a good lawyer and then I'm gonna get the place surveyed. And if there's oil under that good earth I'm gonna sink a well and bring it out for the good of my family.'

Sunshine and Elspeth looked at one another.

'Are you sure you want to do this, Mrs Bartok?' Sunshine asked her. Bethany nodded again.

'I know you two don't want to work the farm. It isn't your style. You might want to open a school or some kind of academy. If I get that black gold out of the ground I can make good use of it for the benefit of the family. After all, it isn't being rich that counts, it's what you do with what you've got. So now that your pa has spoken up good and clear, that's what I aim to do.'

Elspeth looked at Sunshine and smiled.

'Well, if that's the way you and Pa want it then we need to be grateful. But what about Bart?'

Bethany rolled her eyes.

'I don't like to admit this, but truth is I spoiled that boy and if I give him money he'll use it like the Prodigal Son in the Good Book, then come back for more until I'm cleaned right out. So I aim to keep my purse strings tight and if he wants to make himself useful, so much the better for that.'

There's no *happy ever after* ending in this story, since the world is full of trouble and woe. But there are occasional glimpses of sun shining through the clouds. As everyone had suspected there was oil under the Badlands. With good advice and prudence and a lot of support from Elspeth and Sunshine, Bethany was able to set up a company and make herself comparatively rich – rich enough, indeed, to finance an academy in town that became the talk of the whole county.

Elspeth went East again to meet Sunshine's family and train as a teacher, and Sunshine studied art at the same time. When they opened the academy they became quite famous. Sunshine still had his haircut and an occasional shave at The Close Shave, *We Do You Good*. In fact, he became quite friendly with owner Stan Baldock.

One morning while he was sitting in the barber's chair, his friend the barber looked out across Main Street.

'Well I'll be damned, Mr Shining,' he said. 'Well I'll be damned!'

'Not necessarily, Stan, not necessarily,' Sunshine said. The barber pointed across Main Street.

'You see that *hombre* riding past by the saloon over there?'

Sunshine looked across Main Street and saw a man he'd never seen before sitting like a scarecrow on a grey horse. With his unkempt white beard he looked as old as Methuselah. His clothes were dusty and tattered as though he had indeed worn them for centuries.

'Who the hell is that?' Sunshine asked. The barber nodded grimly.

'Well, it's not Old Father Time, though it's hard to tell the difference. No, that's old man Cutaway, the father of those two boys you gunned down.'

'You mean that's their pa?' Sunshine said, aghast.

'That's him,' the barber affirmed. 'He's the last of the big ranchers around these parts. The wives and children of those two Cutaway brothers have disappeared from the face of the earth and nobody knows where they are. Lost his wife and his two sons and now he lives alone in the big ranch house, which is falling apart. They tell me he's quite out of his mind these days. Just shows you how the great ones fall, doesn't, Mr Shining?'

'It sure does,' Sunshine said. 'It sure does.'